I0823477

WHEN WATER BECAME BLUE

ANAÏS BARBEAU-LAVALETTE

translated by RHONDA MULLINS

COACH HOUSE BOOKS, TORONTO

First English-language edition. Original French edition *Femme fleuve* © Marchand de feuilles, 2022.

Conseil des Arts du Canada

ONTARIO ARTS COUNCIL
CONSEIL DES ARTS DE L'ONTARIO
an Ontario government agency
un organisme du gouvernement de l'Ontario

Coach House Books acknowledges the financial support of the Government of Canada for the translation of this book. We are also grateful for the generous assistance for our publishing program from the Canada Council for the Arts, the Ontario Arts Council, and the Department of Canadian Heritage through the Canada Book Fund.

LIBRARY AND ARCHIVES CANADA CATALOGUING IN PUBLICATION

Title: When water became blue / Anaïs Barbeau-Lavalette ; translated by Rhonda Mullins.
Other titles: Femme fleuve. English
Names: Barbeau-Lavalette, Anaïs, author. | Mullins, Rhonda, translator.
Description: Translation of: Femme fleuve.
Identifiers: Canadiana (print) 20250233282 | Canadiana (ebook) 20250233304 | ISBN 9781552455098 (softcover) | ISBN 9781770568716 (EPUB) | ISBN 9781770568709 (PDF)
Subjects: LCGFT: Novels.
Classification: LCC PS8603.A705 F43513 2025 | DDC C843/.6—dc23

When Water Became Blue is available as an ebook: ISBN 978 1 77056 871 6 (EPUB), ISBN 978 1 77056 870 9 (PDF)

Purchase of the print version of this book entitles you to a free digital copy. To claim your ebook of this title, please email sales@chbooks.com with proof of purchase. (Coach House Books reserves the right to terminate the free digital download offer at any time.)

And what is a river anyway? [...]
Immense desire risking its neck.
– Pierre Perrault

I wrap myself around you, like ivy around a stump, like an octopus around its prey. I want to keep you close.

You sharpened my points of attachment to the world. Yet I was already alive.

I didn't need you, and yet you came.

You appear through my window as evening falls. You're wearing a forest-green sweater.

Your shoulders are lifted to the sky to create a frame to protect you.

I know you're not there, but my eyes keep staring into the empty space filled with you, just through the window, just before night.

I know that if I linger, I will smell your scent. I remember it. A sharp, deep aroma, with its source in the hollow of your neck. I know just where to find it. A damp smell, of crystallized honey and sea breeze. But there's something else. I think it's seaweed. A piercing note of your scent, my great love, holds the memories of the shores where we loved each other.

My fingers cling to the wall of an abyss. I'm afraid of the void. I recognize the contours of your cavernous imprint inside me.

I let go of my grip to write you.

I let myself fall here.

The first desirous woman in recorded history is Aspasia. She settled in Athens in 470 BCE. Both cultivated and in love, she held court with Socrates, Pericles, and Sophocles, and was part of the city's intellectual and social life.

A free woman among free men, she was a disruptive force; she was soon relegated to the ranks of prostitute, and history tends to remember her that way. Even though Aspasia was the cultural beating heart of Athens, stories have turned her into a high-ranking courtesan.

While people continue to condemn her morals, they never stop extolling her beauty and intelligence. Aspasia mixed with men, in every way imaginable, and insisted on her right to do so.

But it wasn't until the mid-nineteenth century and *Madame Bovary* that we would read about female desire. Until then, women in literature were either mothers or women of ill repute.

As soon as his novel was published, Gustave Flaubert was accused of offending public and religious morality. Women are merely objects of desire; if desire is to be written, it must be as it is experienced by men.

Women as written receive male desire like a gift, without choosing it, and should they be so bold as to desire in turn, they pay dearly. Madame Bovary commits suicide for having dared to desire.

At the end of the nineteenth century, voices of women authors emerge undercover.

Tired of being denied part of themselves, they take up their pens to reclaim desire. So that female characters experience sexual pleasure and become agents in the received relationship of the desire. *I am not softened marble or if I am marble, it is hot and bad tempered,* wrote Marc de Montifaud in 1878, in reality the intrepid Marie-Amélie Chartroule. Women wrote under male pseudonyms to be read, to be believed. They said: we're not just gentle, we aren't submissive, we are river women; we feel desire and we come longer than you.

Montreal is waking up.

A flock of geese splits the sky.

I point at them like the last miracle, and every time I touch joy.

'GOOD MORNING, LADIES!'

They're returning, and I shout at the sign of our shared spring.

My daughter is embarrassed, squeezes my hand, brings me back down to reality: the bell is about to ring, we have to cross the street. She dons a smile for the crossing guard, greets the adults in the middle of the crosswalk, her little chin lifted high. My daughter is proud. With good reason.

And on the other side of the street, away from all the onlookers, her tender neck stretches toward the V of the flock. Her eyes shine with knowing.

'Welcome, ladies,' she whispers, waving to them.

There are many things I don't understand and many others that seem obvious to me.

Like waving to wild geese.

I choose my alphabet. I teach my daughter how to read the world this way.

I learned to be desired too young.

I learned to desire too late.

Now I know how to get straight to the point.

I've learned upon arriving somewhere to choose a man: the one surrounded by others or the one all on his own; chest puffed out or head tucked under a wing; an explosive laugh or one choked back. What matters most is that he isn't looking at me. That's the essential thing: that he hasn't seen me yet. I'm the one who decides.

I choose him, and I approach him. For an hour or for the night. I examine his folds, the stories his body tells. I explore it, study it. I travel from the corners of his lips to the curve of his eyelashes. I settle into the movement of his hands, the sweetness of his tongue, his choice of words, in the middle of the path of his thoughts.

I choose a man, I discover him, taste him a little or a lot.

It's not a game. It's a way of being alive.

It's my way of reclaiming the right to desire. My way of tearing up all the stories of patient women awaiting the desire of powerful men.

I want to veer into excess and make it a revolution.

To be desirous, like being intelligent, like being tender, like being adventurous.

To be desirous as a character trait.

I have desired above the cows in a tumbledown barn.

I have desired under bridges, with my back against the flaking walls of an alley, and against the handrail of a spiral staircase.

I have desired in front of picture windows overlooking the city or the sea, on tile and hardwood floors.

I have desired against the trunk of a hemlock, a sugar maple, a black spruce.

I have desired on forest moss.

I have desired in dry saunas and steam baths, the bathrooms of trains, planes, and airports.

I have desired in hammocks and canopy beds, in buses, vans, and boats, in lakes and rivers.

I have desired on and under the water.

The places where I have loved form a landscape, a cartography of intimacy, the wandering paths of my attachments.

The river amplifies desire. Its untamed shores are a place for new loves. There's nowhere as steeped in what's wayward and wild as an island.

Without really knowing it, I have loved the river ever since I was little.

The idea of spending a few months on its shores searching for the words to express that love appeals to me.

My man drives me to my summer island exile. We have seen separations before and cultivate the independence of our breath.

We love each other.

Rooted in Sacha's arm, my daughter's hand in the hearth of my hand, I am a tree; my family is my continent.

The beach is crowded that day. The day I see you.

I always dive in all at once. I love provoking encounters. The water takes me at the same time as I take it. Two foreign bodies colliding.

I enter the river eyes closed. I absorb the shock.

I taste the water through my skin. The river is soft, silty, inviting. In its arms, I'm in familiar territory. I understand why some people choose to die in it.

My daughter swims close to me. She's the only one who can keep up. Ama doesn't fear the cold or the opaqueness of the cloudy water. She has learned that the river is our ally. Little air bubbles cling to her long eyelashes like birds to a power line.

Eyes wide open, we cross the fields of sandbars. I have told her that this is the only place we can stare at the sun without burning our eyes. So we open them underwater and look at the giant star behind the delicate wall, the disco ball of our summers, our secret party. It's all it takes to make us want to dance.

On the riverbed, the seaweed has absorbed specks of light, which it reflects back to us.

A four-armed starfish – it seems to have lost an arm – ripples awkwardly, kicks up a curtain of sand and passes through it dancing.

It moves in slow motion, and its rhythm becomes the only rhythm there is.

You're on shore. You're painting.

Things shimmer all around you, but you have eyes only for the river. You're in conversation with it. The two of you have something to resolve.

Your body floats in your long coat, magnificently still. Only your arms are moving, two wings against the wind.

I swim slowly toward you.

Your gestures seem to exist all on their own, thrown out like mooring lines toward the canvas, but what roars inside you can't be neatly tied up. Your dark hair contrasts with the sun and makes it shine brighter, the same sun that carves two windows in your eyes, two little rectangles that dazzle me even from here.

You look like no one else.

I can't take my eyes off your strange presence. You're glued to a world that's not your own.

You seem to have been carved out from another time and set down in this one, which you cling to with the powerful strokes of your brush.

Suddenly you lean toward the river's edge, as if searching for your reflection or someone else's. You try to capture what's under the water's skin. You wait for a surprise, something to emerge, a revelation.

The river spits me out in your face. It's like a birth.

This is where I meet you, between the land and the current.

I want to be your surprise, what emerges, a revelation.

You look at me for a moment, still and stunned. You weren't expecting me.

You stare at me. You decipher me, decode me, make me part of the landscape that had previously been anonymous. You flutter like an aquatic dancer. You signal to me discreetly: don't move. I'm in front of you, half underwater. Your feet are rooted to the ground, and the rest of your body bends like seaweed in the wash. I am the wave.

You snatch lines from the air, and you draw my body emerging from the water.

I step out of the river once your movements slow. I'm already in time with you.

You hold your hand out, confidently pull me toward you. I'm very close now.

You quickly look away from me. It's too much of an encounter all at once.

You hide in my hand, which you're still holding in yours.

With your rounded fingertip, you touch a vein on my hand puffed up from the cold. It winds around my ring finger, crosses the back of my hand, runs up my forearm. Your reading ends there, on the cusp of my elbow. I don't try to hide the shiver than runs through me.

You give me back my hand as if I had dropped it. As if you had just prevented its loss.

I thank you.

You flash a smile.

There's nothing deliberate about you. You don't try to seduce me.

You have the presence of a child, both light and grave.

I want to see what you've painted.

The precise contour of my bones beneath my skin and my curious gaze resting upon you. The long vein that you have just traced throbs bluish-purple on the canvas.

'You saw it from that far away.'

'I sensed it.'

Your voice is calm and intelligent. It warms me.

You look at me without a canvas between us.

Your dark eyes shine like two strokes of fresh paint. There's a spot on the iris of your right eye. A beauty mark that orbits your pupil.

With a careful brushstroke, you add some depth to my blood, then with the same hue, you give life to the waves.

The blue of my vein mixes with the blue of the water.

It wasn't love at first sight. It was an encounter.

It defies explanation; it's the feeling of poetry that takes over our bodies.

The blood vessels in the human body flow for one hundred thousand kilometres.

Or twice around the world.

The *vena amoris* is one of the longest veins in the body. They used to say it connects the ring finger to the heart.

The St. Lawrence River is one of the longest rivers in the country. It flows for 1,197 kilometres and connects the Great Lakes to the Atlantic Ocean.

I catch up with my loved ones on the quay.

They're leaving soon.

Sacha has collected a few samples of aquatic plants he will study later.

He ties a thin ring of wild grass around my finger.

It's pretty.

'Yes. It's pretty and strong.'

It's sea lyme-grass.

He kisses me with his mouth that is always warm and says that sea lyme-grass is precious because it prevents shore erosion.

Sacha and Ama wave to me from the ferry as it leaves.

He's silhouetted against the sky: his chest is an empire, his child-like hair tousled by the wind, his eyes like a cat roaming free in the summer alleys, his arms long like salmon rivers. He knows that I love him from my very roots. He's not afraid of losing me. He knows that I can breathe only with the doors open. He doesn't want to see me die.

With my daughter nestled into his side, he waves, and even from a distance, I can make out his smile. His smile that lets me go. My family disappears.

Part of me disappears with them. A few lines of my silhouette, a change in the pitch of my laugh, a way of looking, feeling, touching. My man and my daughter are of the same soil as me.

I will let go of the mainland.
I will drift toward you.
We will make the river our liquid story.

It's one of the last inhabited islands on the river. Its waters are hard to navigate.

Waves lick the shore like a sugar cube. The island is eroding. Some of its ground is still jutting out, proudly resistant.

The remaining houses were built from wood repurposed from shipwrecks. Their walls hold the memory of the drowned.

Most have been abandoned and sit like pebbles, marking the path to the lighthouse, which rises up defiantly against the sky.

The lighthouse overlooks the shelter of its keepers, sends them beams of light, wears away at them with its caress.

The island's temporary residents share a long inn, a row of modest dens lined up side by side.

I live there, in a room so small I could carry it on my back, in a bundle over my shoulder.

I do a search to find out who you are. I type your name on my keyboard. My fingers on the letters compose it like a whisper, a hideout. I write your name quietly, to keep it a secret. A few photos appear, then images of others who share your first name, as if they had donned the wrong finery. That name is yours. I come across some information about your engineering studies. You learned to build bridges.

There's an old picture of you graduating.

There are paintings. A series of bodies emerging from the water. Women and men, a range of ages, a range of lives, black water up to their thighs. They all seem to come to you. A miraculous catch. An assemblage of reunions.

The lines of your drawings are almost violent in their acuity. Little thrusts of a sword on the canvas. You don't contemplate bodies. You grab them. You seize them. But there is profound gentleness in this precision, a tender attention to your subjects. You're a man who loves.

Your painting seems crystallized in the prism of a childhood.

I remain at a distance to observe you like a baby bird. You have moved closer to the others. They are talking around you. You listen to them. I follow your eyes as they roam over them. You're watching for glimpses of humanity. I know how to spot that from a distance. A quality like a pearl. So rare.

You listen to what they say as you dive under their skin. You say little, you smile. You see an old man take his wife's hand, his bony fingers folding over hers; you see the curious child between his parents digging in the sand down to the water. You read their music, follow their presence with an invisible baton; they become a little animal orchestra you drink in. You get stuck on the gesture of the young woman with a curtain of hair, who brings an errant strap back up to her shoulder. I'm surprised to feel a sharp stab of jealousy. I let it be there; the feeling makes me curious.

You continue your symphony with a toothless old fisherman, accompanying him in a burst of laughter.

You seem hungry for the living, thirsty for their simple beauty. You're attentive to all that emerges; you let it penetrate you; your whole body is an open window. I draw closer. I want to follow myself into you.

It's still hard to lay claim to female desire, but love is the exclusive domain of women.

They take more of an interest in it than men do, and rightly so.

If maternity has long conditioned the recognition of the social existence of women, later on love gave them a right to a history, if not to History. After the era of saints, then of queens, it is as beloveds or as women-in-love that women get spoken about, that their existence is the subject of a story, which appeared with the novel.

As Mona Chollet clearly explains, in a sense women owe their 'existence' to love.

I, too, have existed to please.

I was subjugated, a handmaid to the feeling of love.

It took many encounters – with men, with women – to lead me back to myself. Toward a joyful awareness of my power.

Today, I can desire whenever I like. It's not a need; it's a resource.

An extension of myself.

Encounters stretch me, open me, spread me wide.

I don't distinguish desire from love.

Obviously, there are minor passing desires, fleeting like hot flashes.

But why separate true desire from the love it invokes?

Loving desire is rare. It's a celebration of the other, a joint creation.

I desire you, therefore I love you. I can't come without my heart.

Alone on the shore, standing in front of the river, your body splits the sky in two, drawn gently into the little square of your canvas. You paint the water and the outline of the village in the distance, which appears to be floating on it. I already recognize your sharp gestures as a staccato breath of air; you chase the waves, your brow furrowed and your eyes burning.

They are so black, your eyes.

You put down your brush when I approach.

You ask whether I slept well. Whether I wrote well.

You really want to know; you're expecting an answer, not just a social convention.

I slept little and wrote nothing.

'You?'

You throw the small half-painted square into the grey water, which rejects it too, sending the nascent painting back onto the deserted shore.

You're trying to paint the river, but you can't. It's stronger than you.

So far, you've managed to paint only an inhabited river. Crowned with a halo of what shines in the distance or with a human springing from the waves.

The river alone, the river as entity, defeats you.

You don't know how to bring it to life.

You look at your hands. They are a map of all the blues in the world, and none seems to be the right one.

I tell you that if you were to paint the river on its own, it would have to be your encounter with it.

It would be just the two of you. Painting the river alone would speak of you.

I'm bothering you.

You scratch at all the blues that are starting to dry on your hands. It's like you're carrying a thousand seas in your palms. You make me thirsty.

You grab your brush, and with an abrupt gesture, you add a flash of azure to me. You think blue suits me. I thank you. I've been told that before.

Your brush is named for its shape, a whale's tail. It comes alive.

You play on my skin, and the marine mammal takes possession of my neck. You trace a path of wild waves on it.

Its touch is as light as summer, and my body receives it solemnly.

You aren't shy being here. You flow along the projections of my collarbones, you wander along the path of my veins, your brush climbs all the different grains of my skin. You read my neck, you recite my manubrium. You teach me its name. A little triangular land that seems so fragile, this piece of skeleton that reminds me that I am mortal. You love it. You settle into it.

I let my dams break. I let myself drop under the water.

Philosophers have given desire a bad name.

Plato, Lucretius, Epicurus, Socrates: for every single one of them, desire is a millstone to thought, shackles to reflection.

Eros, god of desire, fell in love with a mere mortal; desire therefore arises from a lack, a hollow, a void to fill.

But it strikes me that this lack magnificently defines our species.

It's what draws me toward the person I don't know, the person I'm not. Boundaries can be obliterated by mere movement.

If I don't feel the lack, I remain immobile and static.

I'm alive and mobile, and I reach toward you.

A woman dives in front of us.

She's swallowed by the river, which erases any trace of her. There's no ring remaining to say she was there; the water's surface returns to its initial folds, the heavy blanket of the river hides the fisherwoman, who becomes a secret.

My notebook lies open like a body on display; it's waiting for me to set words to its paper. I would like to write the river, but I'm absorbed by you.

But you don't steal the limelight from any part of the landscape; naturally humble, you blend in with what surrounds you. You have the same inner dignity as the land; you share its melancholy.

I feel like I have known you for a long time. Something in your centre makes me want to celebrate.

You paint with your head down.

You look like you're doing battle, but you're dancing.

The lower part of your body draws the river toward it, drawn magnetically, as if to a woman's waist while dancing.

Many have tried to capture the water's movement and colour. Turner, whom you admire, was tied to the mast of a sailing ship in the belly of a storm to meet it and try to reproduce it. His body lashed to the top of the ship, taking the wind head on, the breaking waves whipping his face, he became, for a time, the ocean. He was no longer merely a spectator of the world; he was part of it. He was in the painting.

He painted *Snow Storm* by spitting the sea back up and almost died doing it.

Your gestures gradually slow. Your brush is less busy. I feel like your breath is calming too. I have closed my notebook to better see you.

You tell me about Courbet, whose only work I'm familiar with is *L'Origine du monde* and the boldness of female genitals painted in close-up.

You tell me that the painter sat in front of a window on the Breton coast and immortalized the stormy sea as no one ever had. The ocean became the sole subject: no shipwreck, no sunset, an event in itself.

The green waves grow angry and break, raging, and enter the Musée d'Orsay.

You stop. You come over. You seem suddenly cautious. Something has just made you fragile. Maybe it's me.

You sigh. You need shelter.

I feel there's no place that's right for you. That your lunar skin is made of porcelain. You're a set of china from the nineteenth century, and you take the risk of sitting down beside me.

Like me, you feel we're under threat. I won't be your shelter.

We look out at the white water together. It makes us seem even more still. You smile. Little lines form around your eyes, like roads that lead to your gaze. I want to travel them all. I want to kiss your eyelids. You feel it. You turn to me. I drink in the dark water of your eyes while you talk to me about blue, which absorbs you. Then I slip toward your lips.

The idea of becoming the colour blue crosses my mind the moment I see the word form on your mouth, your moist lips coming together to say 'blue.'

You tell me that blue has not always belonged to the sea. The colour was long scorned, and it was the purer green that represented water.

But people eventually wanted to distinguish the lakes from the forests on the world maps being drawn. So, to avoid confusing them with trees, the oceans became blue. The abandoned colour was rehabilitated: men and women wanted to wear the look of the open sea. The dye race accelerated. Lands previously ignored suddenly became precious; they concealed the new gold: lapis lazuli, sold to rich countries to extract the illumination of the sea.

Your voice vibrates in your torso and storms your mouth, before sweeping like the mistral between your red lips.

I fill myself up with you while you go on, enamoured with the story of a colour.

Fields of indigo grow everywhere. American slaves' fingers turned blue as they harvested the flowers.

A dye maker in Berlin discovers that by mixing cow's blood with calcined potash a vibrant blue results, which painters couldn't wait to get their hands on: Prussian blue.

The market for blue explodes as people try to capture the watery depths in colour. The world's surface is a matter of hues as much as textures. Artists keep trying and despair: they want to be faithful to the landscapes but struggle to capture them.

Darwin drew inspiration from *Werner's Nomenclature of Colours* to describe the sea: 'Indigo with a little Azure blue,' haloed with a 'Prussian blue' sky, mixed with ultramarine.

Science still rubbed shoulders with art at the time, and to properly capture the world, one had to be familiar with its colours. This urgent quest for the right tone is testimony to a moving, fragile link between nature and people.

In trying to paint the river, you try to encounter it.

I like your mind.

The things you know excite me. Your knowledge is erotic.

I run away.

I gather my notebook and my desire with both hands. It's the first time I have ever retreated.

I move away to watch you from afar. You're standing erect, alert before the horizon, like a star pupil before the teacher.

I think you're strange. I think you're magnificent.

'See you tomorrow!'

I know full well why you scare me.

You shout out to me, 'See you tomorrow,' and already I'm waiting for you forever.

I put my books on the bed; they're like life preservers. I lie down on my belly, and my body clears a path between their stories. I've collected the writings I've found about islands; their authors tried to write the water, choppy or calm.

Melville, Sciascia, Baricco, Hugo.

Jacques Roumain. All water is connected, right down to tears, and Jacques Roumain doesn't write about the river or the sea. He writes about the dew and the island where he was born, Haiti, dried up. He writes about a battle to find the spring of running water to save his people. Manuel and Annaïse will govern the dew together. They will make it spring from the earth once again. People will die. There will be tender, carnal love. And water like a new miracle.

Around us, the hungry water is rising, ravaging the shore.

Through the window, the lonely lighthouse raises its hand. It has long been asking the river the same question, which answers with its silent roar.

Only two people understand this dialogue. Clo, the lighthouse keeper, whose body is smooth as driftwood, and his wife, Yvonne. They live here, bent over the seed of the waves or pulled toward the clouds. Never between the two. The line that separates the sky from the sea scares them; they've learned that's how you die. Their lined eyes tell of stormy nights spent scanning the horizon to prevent shipwrecks.

They are two of the few people who know about the ghost islands offshore. The islands that come and go with the tides. They're out there, their rock heads emerging from the water; they appear on maps and tell the tale of solitary explorers. But whenever a delegation sails to find and explore them, they disappear.

They are free, moving islands, the river's companions, with no lighthouse or mooring lines.

I close my eyes. I'm a ghost island.

I break on your glass neck, on your protruding spine, on the wave of your breath. I come apart on your lips that say 'blue.' I get caught in the taut net of your saliva; I hide in the depths of your salty waters, behind your eddies; I govern your dew; I come.

I hear the door next to mine squeak as it opens. My neighbour's footsteps in the next room.

I hear her wet feet. It's like she's bringing the river back with her.

She dove until she reached night.

I open my door, and we exchange a look, a neighbourly greeting, a small courtesy bridge so we don't sleep alone.

She invites me over. She has wine.

My next-door neighbour was born on the Shima Peninsula in Japan. She undresses in her perfectly ordered room, asks me to dry her back, and pours me a glass of Syrah.

She apologizes: the wine is warm.

I wipe the water from the curve of her shoulder blades. Her muscles are all beating as one, like an orchestra.

I take three swigs in a row. It prickles and dries the roof of my mouth; the wind from the estuary blows in and makes itself at home. I feel good.

'Have a seat.'

There are no chairs, and the cramped space leaves me few options.

I settle in cross-legged on her bed. I'm in a cloud of the scent of her sweat.

Hisaé leaves her wet clothes on the floor. The hours of work are over. She stretches, she drinks, she yawns loudly; Hisaé is a tomcat.

She tells me that she grew up on the shores of the river, not far from here. She's an archeologist. She's interested in the traces we leave behind. She's searching underwater for human relics. She has found treasures before. A cod fisherman's watch from the nineteenth century and a French officer's silverware. But Hisaé's favourite things are submerged quays.

Her cheeks flush with each sip. She whispers that the water holds and protects a society's unconscious. Its forgotten stories.

'Did you know that the northern half of the island is already underwater?'

I didn't know.

Hisaé pours me another glass.

Several homes are already submerged. And the village church, too.

Hisaé bursts into haughty laughter upon seeing my disbelief. She tells me to go swimming there, assures me there are miracles to see.

As she talks, Hisaé pulls spines from her fingers.

She didn't find anything today, but she fished.

Hisaé fishes urchins with her bare hands. Fish is sold by weight. She's in a race: the men are all in their twenties, with the hearts of mildly deranged seamen; they are junkies of adrenaline and of the deep. When they emerge from the water, a little vein pulses on their necks, the jugular, the one that attracts vampires.

Hisaé wants to bite them. Sometimes she holds back. Sometimes she doesn't.

She's greedy, like me.

The young seadogs place bets on her. They no longer include her in their predictions. She's in a class all her own: she dives between cigarettes, she fishes urchins with her bare hands, she has spines in her palms, and she likes it.

They think she's either crazy or brave. They respect her, that much she knows.

'You have red-wine lips.'

Hisaé leans toward me and licks my mouth.

Her tongue is broad and coarse; her tongue prickles. Her tongue is punk.

Before I leave, I tell her I'm not afraid of spines either. I collect cacti. They're untouchable, so I touch them.

I collect outcasts. Cacti and others. I find them a warm place. It's a vestige of my past. Some of the pieces of my story were never glued back on; abandoned bodies orbit around me.

So I caress cacti.

Through the window, the sky has grown overcast.

I look to the north. I imagine a steeple standing under the black river, living down below.

I walk through the underbrush that leads to the lighthouse. Hisaé trails me slowly, a thermos of coffee in her hand.

Ten or so little silhouettes are visible at the tip of the island. I recognize you among them; you are taller and the only one looking at me.

A point in my stomach is connected to yours, and I advance, magnetized, as if I have no say in the matter.

Hisaé lets me speed up without her and inhabits each of her heavy steps like an argument: nothing and no one will alter her trajectory.

Your scent reaches me before I reach you. My chest constricts then expands as if taking flight, but I choose to remain on the ground, with you, and I station myself at your side.

Hisaé watches and winks at me in amusement.

She's a fourteen-year-old in the body of a big boss.

You stand erect next to me, and your calm seeps into me.

You whisper that I still have a brushstroke of muted blue, right there. An anchor point for my manubrium.

I tell you I'm keeping it. It's your signature, and I like it.

That makes you happy.

I want it to last.

I know I could make it last.

Clo, the lighthouse keeper, clears his throat. He isn't a great orator, so instead he has put on his good shirt. His hands shoved in his pockets, he thanks us for visiting the island, which in a way he considers his own.

He glances at the old lighthouse.

At the rate the river is rising, it won't be here long.

Encased in an orange windbreaker from the last century, Yvonne takes over from him. Her skin is weathered from the wind, and her body is worn out from babies. They had seven, right here on the island. Seven little islanders who grew up with their chests to the northeast wind.

This island is their old turtle.

It has held Clo and Yvonne all their lives, and they have watched over it in return. They have been through its winters, rocked themselves to the rhythm of the ice, scanning the wake of ocean liners.

Together they epitomize what's most beautiful about our species: watching, day and night, over their kind without their kind realizing. They don't want medals; anonymity is what makes their success. When they had to go out, it was to save bodies from the waves. And then there was often a surprising catch.

Yvonne said that a shipment of flour clothed her family for over a year. She cut out rough little overalls from the jute bags they fished out, which were durable enough for children.

A few years later, a shipment of jam spilled into the river. It was a sweet year.

Now the lighthouse is automated, and the day-to-day tasks are streamlined.

The Ministry of Wildlife has asked the old couple to keep a bird log, to track changes in populations.

Clo and Yvonne walk the island several times a day, taking small steps and counting the terns, songbirds, and brown pelicans.

Attracted by the brightness of the lighthouse, birds often slam into its walls. Whenever he can, Clo patches them up. He knows how to make a wing splint out of matches.

But when the bird is too broken, he leaves it to die in the warmth in front of the fireplace, in a Converse shoebox that his grandchildren decorated with old images from *National Geographic*. Hyenas, kangaroos, and bald eagles paper the little makeshift coffin. With the wisdom of a six-year-old, Irène says they will welcome the casualty on the other side. Dying is probably easier when you know someone is expecting you.

Clo holds Yvonne's hand. They are firmly planted in each other. She is so large, and he is so frail, clinging to the same centre. Attached to the rocky back of their old turtle.

The couple reassures me. In keeping company with the lighthouse, I'm convinced its keepers have inherited a bit of its light. Or the reverse. Clo and Yvonne glow in the dark.

Their little land is disappearing; that is its fate as an island. Soon all that will be left will be scattered, unstable memories. The lighthouse keepers don't get to decide what should be preserved, and the powers that be will find no memories to share here. Not many objects will end up in a museum.

With a bit of luck, a few will find their way into eternity. A captain's compass or a sailor's wooden pipe. But the bowl their wives used to cook and the needle that mended the nets will be forgotten. That aspect of daily life doesn't interest us.

The memories of women can just stay drowned.

You tell me to follow you. We go to the northern tip and pass by a few ghost houses on the way.

A golden house is perched at the river's edge, as if it were holding its breath before diving. You break the rusted lock that holds its wooden door closed without conviction.

We head into the belly of the abandoned house. It smells like old books. The humidity has rippled the yellow wallpaper. I've always loved old wallpaper. It has the same effect on me as a picnic blanket in the middle of a field. Both are testimony to a careful attention to beauty, even fleeting.

Dead birds are scattered on the floor. They were held prisoner for too long and couldn't find their way back to the chimney entrance. You collect the cadavers stiffened by the salt air and erect a little pyramid of flightless wings.

A rickety table sits in the middle of the kitchen. The patterns of plastic doilies have left their mark. You can almost hear the missing people slurping their soup. And it sounds like a loud *shlsss*, and it sounds like a loud *shlsss*...

Three fishing rods lean against the fireplace, the kettle is waiting on the stove, a wall clock runs for no one. A basket of shiny plastic fruit, a pink *Frozen* school bag, a few pieces of Lego, a drawing of a smiling jellyfish hanging on the door of the open fridge.

A clean rectangle on the ground, an imprint on the dusty floor.

'They took the piano.'

A family of fishers with no fishing rods but with a piano.

What we keep says as much as what we leave behind.

You go upstairs. The floor creaks under your feet.

They took their bed and abandoned the bedspread on the floor.

You open the window with a silent, confident gesture. The material world yields to you. You have the conciliatory hand of those who make things.

The water stopped right here.

The area around the house has been swallowed up.

The river is carving out the land and expanding its bed.
The thin, moth-eaten curtains dance in the sea breeze.
You stare at them as they flutter.

I sit on the floor, near you.
Waves slap against the wall of the house.
We could slowly founder with it.
We don't touch each other; we brush against each other.
Our need to be together is in the air and the water, between our gestures and under our skin.
You check your watch.
I can't imagine what you can be waiting for other than time.
You pull a notebook and a pencil from your bag; you sketch the movement of the white curtains.
I do as you do. I don't want anything but you.
I write you while you draw.
Our gestures drift and align like those of the animals.
You look at your watch again.
You say, 'Listen,' and I listen.
At first, I hear only you. Your pulse, your rhythm, your presence that seeps into me.
Then, the bells. Distant, muted, underwater.
It's noon. The damaged bell tower rings in slow motion.
I rest my head against yours.
The presence of water makes us appreciate the land.
Our thoughts touch each other and swarm.

It's not in the magnetizing of our skin.
I don't immediately want to be in your arms or to put my tongue on your sex.
What binds me to you is mainly on the inside.
I feel woven to your twists and turns; our labyrinths lead to each other. I get lost where you are lost.
We are made of the same stuff.

We can't resist becoming entangled.

From now on, the days exist just for the two of us.

The air is salty. A beam of light slices through the forest. I put on an oversized sweatshirt; I don't want anything to contain my flesh. The tips of my breasts rub on the soft fabric. I take off my shoes. A grey hare perches on its hind legs.

Its ears slant toward us, like arrows. A direct hit.

I pick a few tendrils of lichen, which I bring to our mouths.

It crunches between the teeth.

Lichen is what results when algae meet fungi.

In the nineteenth century, the connection between the two could be imagined only as a parasitic one. The idea that they might rely on each other for their existence was unimaginable.

At the time, a faulty idea of Darwinism reigned. People assumed that the only type of relationship possible was one of competition. The individual is a fortress that needs no one to stand.

But lichen is neither plant nor fungi nor algae. It's a symbiosis between two species, crossing boundaries. The fungi lick the cells of the algae, which open up to receive it. It snakes between them, and the two species fuse to become something new: lichen.

We leave the forest.

The water lies before us.

River rocks dot the shore with a dazzling green, and some, wearing lichen dresses, punctuate the landscape with bright yellow.

We arrive at an inlet. The rocks form a cove, where a tongue of water stretches out lazily. Its stone jaw separates us from the beach.

'In the Balkans every year, pickers collect tons of lichen, to extract the absolute from the moss. It's used as a base in perfumery.'

I turn around then.

I felt your heat on my neck, and I know you just breathed me in with your eyes.

You unfold your easel and take a blank canvas from its leather case.

'Lichen is also a colour. You can use its acids to make hues of blue.'

You stare at the river, as if you're declaring war on it.
It's the only thing you look at this way.

Blue is a precious colour. For millennia, artists' palettes had few hues, but almost all the colours: red, yellow, green, brown, black, and white. All that was missing was blue. There was a simple reason for that: there are very few blue minerals, and extremely rare are those that retain their power to dye once reduced to powder.

It was in the second century BCE, in Turkmenistan, that someone managed to grind lapis lazuli to extract a blue mineral, lazurite, which could be used as a pigment. It would be given the pretty name of 'ultramarine.'

The colour would reach Mediterranean painters only in the eighth century.

Blue would remain rare and hard to find, and only specialized dyers would venture to use it. There were strict rules among holders of the secrets of colours: a dyer of yellows couldn't make red or purple, and especially not blue. Playing around in another's colour was punishable by a heavy prison sentence. To each their own secrets; to each their own colour.

While carefully mixing yours, you tell me your story of what prompted Picasso's Blue Period.

On February 17, 1901, the young artist, at the time barely twenty years old, is sitting at the terrace of the Hippodrome Café, near Montmartre. Pablo is a close friend of the painter Carles Casagemas. They spend their time with women they have dance for them and whose portraits they paint.

Carles is madly in love with Germaine, a vivacious young woman, whom he wants for himself. But Germaine is a free agent, and Carles is in pain.

The sun is blazing despite the dampness; discussions mingle with bursts of laughter. Casagemas points a gun at his mistress and fires. Germaine doesn't die, not that day, but her unhappy lover puts the gun to his head and kills himself in the middle of winter, after two swigs of absinthe.

A few drops of blood land in Pablo's glass. The blood mixes with the water from the ice. Pablo takes his final swig, and it starts to snow.

Once home, he takes out all his blues and enters a dark, sad, melancholic period.

Pablo would paint primarily in blue for four years. In many hues of blue, which came to represent his tears.

I would have liked to have known Germaine, the free woman who survived a man's madness that day. Germaine, Pablo Picasso's blue muse.

For you, blue is neither gloomy nor sad. Blue is luminous; it's the opposite of death.

I'm stretched out in my adolescent lair, filled with a deliberate mess: I want to take advantage of everything that solitude affords me, chaos included.

I continue my reading on lichen to stay close to you. I don't know whether I'm algae or fungi, but I feel viscerally enamoured of what you're made of.

I read that we have already sent a specimen of lichen into space.

Hurtling at breakneck speeds, thousands of kilometres from its home, the fusion of algae and fungi was brought home two weeks later.

The lichen had survived temperatures ranging from −190 to 90 degrees. A first.

I would like to take a long voyage with you.

I also read that, in the past, some forms of lichen were thought to heal heartbreak. But this lichen was rare: it grew only on the skulls of the hanged. That's where the brave collected it. The most cunning resold it at a high price, lining their pockets with the sorrow of others.

My daughter pulls me out of the macabre. She's good at that. Ama is a seasoned degloomifier, a professional of joy. She calls to me over the hanged.

Holding the phone much too close to her face, she walks me through the house, glued to her great big eyes: I visit her bedroom, which is as messy as mine; I meet her families of crayons, her families of rocks, her families of ants; I help her braid the cat's fur; I count three basketball dribbles; I lose at Rock Paper Scissors, and I follow her finger tracing the path of the raindrops on the window pane.

She explains that after they fall, the drops go back up into the clouds, then they fall again to fill the river and the oceans, before 'epavorating' again.

'That's the way it's been forever and ever. Things that never end are beautiful, aren't they, Maman?'

Ama learned about the rain cycle in school.

She tells me that aaallll water goes back into the clouds before falling back down on us. Even tears.

'Yes, yes, tears, too, Maman.'

I hear: 'Ama, dinner's ready.'

Sacha is standing between two steaming colanders.

Ama plunges her hands into the steam.

Some of her tears may be on the head of broccoli.

Sacha is handsome. An orchestra conductor with expansive gestures. A sturdy oak. A fall bouquet.

He sets the table and tells me about his seedlings, the greenhouse extension, the azalea bulbs, and the blue poppies – 'go wash your hands' – then he moves on to registering Ama for swimming lessons, changing a lock, Ama's drawing of a hippocampus that she will give to Janine, whom she loves and who is losing her memory.

'We're going to eat.'

'Enjoy your dinner, my loves.'

'Enjoy your dinner, Maman.'

I leave them to their dinner for two.

Silence is always thicker after hearing the voices of your beloveds.

It's always a little darker after their light too.

And yet I don't want to be sitting with them right now.

The flicker of my candle suits me nicely.

My exile is precious.

I undo my sea-lyme-grass wedding band and slip it in my pocket.

I free my *vena amoris*, my vein of love; I erode a little, I open a pack of rusks and a beer.

A slim figure is silhouetted against the shore. She undresses, believing she is hidden from view, or not caring.

She puts on a wetsuit, sits down to put on flippers.

I recognize her youth, her matte skin, and her thick hair, which she tosses with a light gesture.

I watch you watch her. I want to know everything that interests you: I go to join you in the shade that's about to meet the water, over there.

She turns as I approach. She lifts her mask, revealing two huge eyes of soot so dark they cast a shadow. Even the pupil disappears in them. I don't quite know where to look at this woman, who is happily greeting me.

Her name is Narcisse. It's her real name: her parents are Iranian. She's a biologist studying underwater forests.

She points to the river, a darker area, about thirty metres from shore.

'There's one right there. Do you want to see it?'

Yes, very much so.

The young woman pulls a second mask from her bag, the way a biker would pull a second helmet from under the seat of her bike. She invites me to go for a ride.

We make our way through the cold river, and I encounter the joy that bubbles to the surface only here, the moment my body slips into the water, all at once.

I wonder why you always want to paint blue. Everything around us is green.

My heart rate slows, my breathing too.

Narcisse swims alongside me. She advances almost without undulating her body; she embraces the movement of the water.

There are hardly any witnesses to our passing. A motionless crab, suddenly alerted by our presence. A few mussels clumped together share a secret.

Narcisse points to a lazy jellyfish, who leads the way.

It pulsates in front of us like a kindly flashing light.

Some jellyfish are immortal. They must be heavy with all the stories they hold.

Narcisse has moved ahead and is now swimming alongside the jellyfish. I feel like they understand each other. Narcisse speaks many languages.

I see it. The forest. Tall seaweed rises up from the sand and waves its way toward the surface, each piece on its own, yet in harmony with the group. The seaweed is beautiful. A gang of girls on the dance floor. Rays of light pierce the water and slip among the plants, winding around their waists, brushing against their legs that just won't quit.

There's red, orange, yellow here, too, in addition to the green.

And I hear a new sound, the sound of quiet bubbles, conversation at the end of the evening.

I've lost Narcisse in the middle of the dance floor.

I'm alone in the underwater forest, and I fear nothing, not even staying here.

But I want to go back to tell you about the colours I've seen.

I find Narcisse entwined in a copse of seaweed, which she's gently untangling with slow, practiced gestures. She has taken a small tool from her pocket and draws each piece of seaweed toward her by the waist, bends and dips it in a slow waltz, then punctures the tip of a leaf.

She smiles at me from behind her mask, signals that she's almost done.

She releases her catches, which start waving again, a new beam passing through their skin.

We return to the surface.

Our heads pop out of the water, and it's like arriving in a new country.

'Everything okay?'

I remove my mask and my snorkel.

I smile at Narcisse. I feel like I just left a party I wasn't invited to, but where I was expected nonetheless.

I look to the shore.

You're there. You're tiny, but you fill the space.

The wind is up. I shiver.

Narcisse gets undressed on the beach. She's magnificent.

I ask her what she's measuring underwater.

Seaweed breathes. It stores carbon. Narcisse is monitoring the respiration of the forests.

She perforates the seaweed to identify it. It's like she's giving it a name. She will visit it regularly, track its changes over the course of the summer.

Narcisse observes the reaction of the seaweed to hypoxia. It's a beautiful word, like a precious metal. It means the river's asphyxia as it loses oxygen. What used to live in it now dies, or moves on, biding its time.

Aquatic forests react to hypoxia. Some try to flee. Others breathe harder. Still others hold their breath.

This's what Narcisse is studying.

She offers me a cigarette.

'And you? What are you looking for?'

'… I write.'

But I don't yet know how to talk about the river. It intimidates me.

'You have to start with the effect it has on you.'

With a burst of laughter, Narcisse tells me she's sleeping with the river while she waits for Jonas.

'That way, the same waters penetrate us, and I can sort of touch him.'

Jonas paddles an ice canoe to break the ice. He's on a mission to capture an iceberg and tow it to the Canary Islands, where the land is drying up; the people too.

A 30-million-tonne block of ice would provide 30 billion litres of water. It would give over five hundred thousand inhabitants drinking water for a year.

In territorial waters, icebergs are under state jurisdiction, but in the high seas, they are *res nullius* and become the property of the person who takes control of them, just like a shipwreck.

Jonas is waiting for the pack ice to break up and release his iceberg. He will hunt it with a harpoon.

Narcisse is in love with a cowboy.

The only one of my grandmother's paintings I managed to salvage from oblivion is the story of collapse.

Large black blocks emerge from a white background. The river erupts.

It was painted in 1960, eight years after she abandoned her children. My mother was eleven at the time; her aunts, Janine and Pauline, sent her to a boarding school for a while, where she counted the hours until the weekend. Then she could finally play hopscotch and eat cinnamon butter.

I address the river like a confidante. It's always moving, too, on its way somewhere, elusive.

If all waters talk to each other, its waters knew the woman who fled. This is where she sought refuge after leaving her two children. The river gave her cover, offered her the excuse of the open sea. She reinvented herself as a mail carrier on its shores and fed on the bodies of men passing through. They were a dotted line in her emotional landscape; they traced a carnal road and made her feel like she was alive.

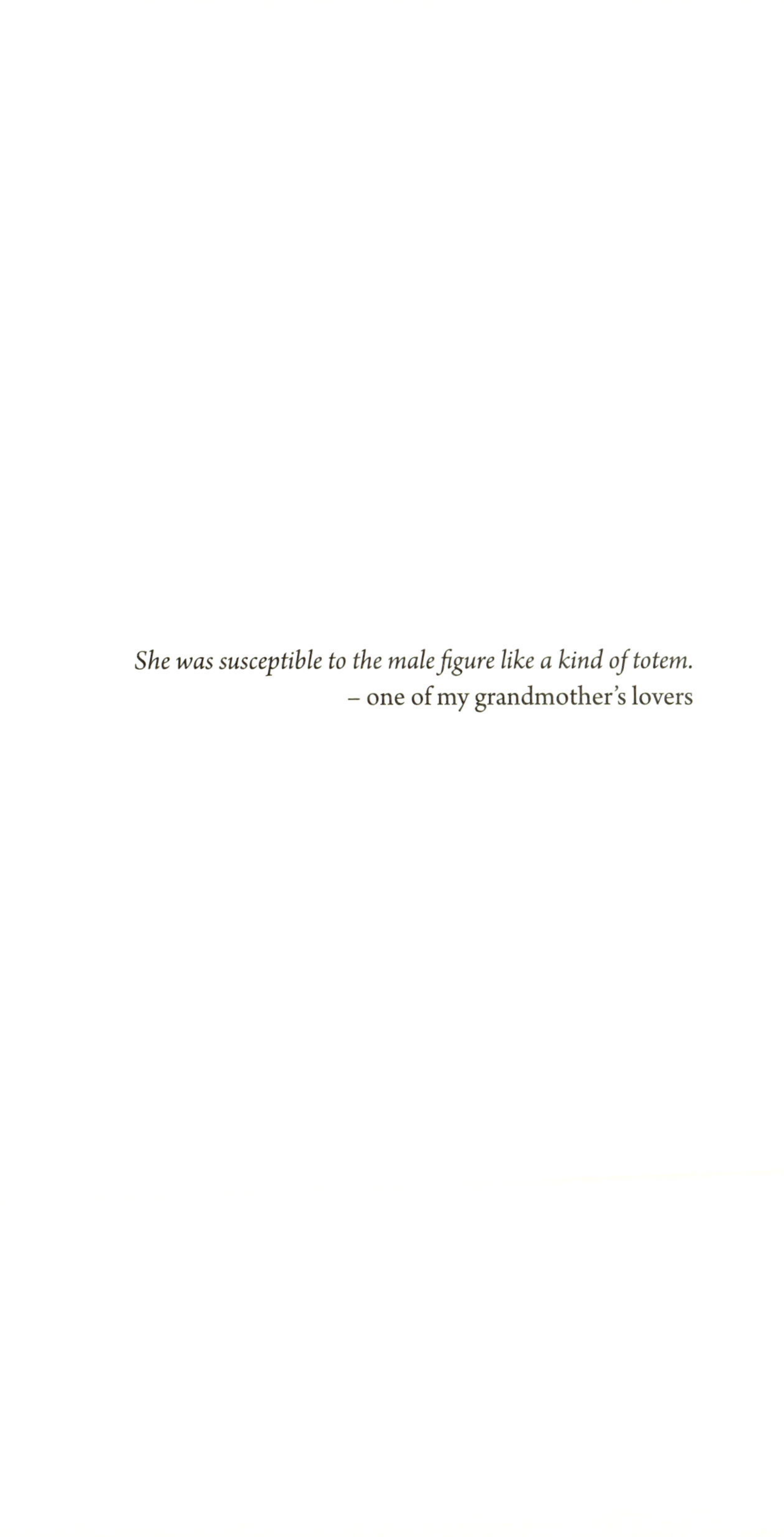

She was susceptible to the male figure like a kind of totem.
– one of my grandmother's lovers

There used to be giant ocean liners that carried unwanted children and those no one could take care of. They would dock for a few hours, and mothers would come to place their little ones in wooden compartments, where they travelled, neatly stowed, to another place, where they would be better fed, where people were willing to watch over them as they grew.

Hundreds of infants, in a vertical line, like lower case *i*'s ad infinitum. A wet nurse pitching on the same waves as the babies made sure they survived.

They say some babies were swaddled in half of a torn apron. Their mothers, who were often illiterate, hoped that one day they would find their other half. They say it was those babies, nourished by the invisible hope of reunion, who were most likely to survive the voyage.

I thank Narcisse for the dive.

Jonas will return with the cold weather to study the ice around her.

'But you, what do you do in winter?'

'I wait for him on shore.'

'So, basically, you wait for him all the time.'

'Yes. It suits me.'

Narcisse is desiring a presence, rather than grieving an absence.

She packs up her equipment and, before heading off to explore the southern tip of the island, she shows me her hole punch: the tip is in the shape of a heart.

'I used to mark the seaweed with just a circle, but it was hard to find it afterwards. Holes form naturally in forests. But not hearts.'

While her man awaits a collapse, Narcisse pierces hearts on the dance floor of an underwater forest.

I feel you moving in the distance. You walk toward me.

As she leaves, Narcisse shouts that she knows I liked it. She could tell.

But not to venture into the forest alone, ever.
'You could be caught in a net!'

As I watch you approach, I realize I already am.

You come to me. You join me on the shore. I was too far out. I was underwater.

It scared you.

Were you afraid of losing me?

Your hand on the nape of my neck. Your fingers on my skin. I simply receive you. I close my eyes to better dilute myself in the sensation. I let my modesty drop like I would a piece of clothing. It seems to have been invented for this very moment, for this perfect moment when I abandon it.

I take your painted thumb in my mouth. I swallow all your blues – cyan, petroleum blue, royal blue, Majorelle blue, and teal. Your skin feels new inside me, and I am discovering your flavour. You taste of salt, leather, and sweat. Your thumb is an animal I swallow, and you offer me your lips. Your inner flesh, vulnerable, scratchable.

Your saliva burns. I taste the hidden face of your cheeks, the roundness of your tongue. I don't know who is flowing into whom; the frame of the day disappears, and I dive into the surrounding night. A first kiss in quicksand, like a terrifying surprise; I didn't know it was possible. We're too much in tune. We're already sinking into each other. This is going to hurt.

You keep trying to paint the water, but you refuse to touch it. I can't write by sight alone. I need to encounter things with my body. I invite you again: 'Come on!'

But you deny yourself the water. You don't want to take the plunge.

You cling to the world with your eyes and that's enough.

I tell you that you have to touch, that vision is a passive way of perceiving the world.

You tell me that's not true. That vision engages. That beauty is born from a tacit agreement between what is looked at and who is looking, an encounter between the eye and the object.

You add a bit more magenta to the primary blue on your palette. Then a bit of white, and you mix it. It's pretty, but you aren't satisfied. No blue is your blue.

Touch used to dictate how we perceived the world. It was through our hands, through the body, through contact, that we probed its roughness. We were a manual civilization, able to identify through touch the modulations in what was around us. I plunge my hands into your black beard. It tells a different story than if I had just looked at it, and no one can convince me otherwise. Your black beard is coarse like the first cutting of wheat, dense like a wild forest. I want to lick the skin beneath it; I want to lick everything you hide. Your black beard sharpens my fingers, hones my senses; it speaks to me of your sex and the sex of all the others before you. My fingers roam through your beard, and I touch a piece of your powerful virility.

Your beard makes me wet as you look me in the eye.

I remember an online presentation by Arthur Lochmann, a French philosopher turned carpenter, who talked about the importance of learning to touch again.

I liked his story, the story of a scholar who walked away from academia to work with wood and refine his reflections on the world. A philosopher of the real. But his talk was rather austere, the young man quite shy and tired in front of his screen. There were a number of listeners, all invisible, and I was falling asleep when a spectacle that could only belong to this still-fragile modernity roused me. An audience member had forgotten to mute her mic. When she spoke, her image replaced that of the philosopher, interrupting his talk on the importance of touch. The audience member and her name, Corrine S., appeared without her realizing. Corrine S. had a little girl in her arms, who had come for a kiss. We heard the mother say, in the softest voice ever, 'I love you, my darling. Sleep tight,' wrapping her arms around her child as if drinking a glass of water.

Her arms around her daughter and her cheek against hers: the essence of tenderness.

Then the screen switched back to Arthur Lochmann, who, like the other participants, had been interrupted. He hesitated a moment, perhaps also tempted to bid the child good night. Corrine S. was listening once again, unaware of the shift in tone she had just created.

The learned man smiled for the first and last time.

Corrine S.'s warmth, her arms around her child, had pierced the austerity of thoughts and the coldness of screens.

For a moment, we were truly together.

Of the entire talk on the importance of touch, what I remember most was Corrine S. touching her little darling.

In the late afternoons in my regular life, Ama lies down on me as if I were a beach. Ever since she was little, this is where she has washed up. She drifts off, she sweats, she drools on my skin, and I absorb her droplets, which make me grow. Before she arrived, I was always thirsty.

Her capacity for love is gargantuan; I struggle to understand where she draws it from, if mine comes from her. Maybe it's like the water cycle. It goes round and round. I charge myself in her, and she charges in me.

Ama's pulse beats in her neck. Blue washes through her little protruding vein. The metronome of my life beats there.

My man comes into the bedroom when night falls, his fingers black with soil. He brings a new branch to our noses, analyzes the odours of honey and linden, decodes the nuances of night-blooming jasmine, which releases its fragrance only at night, kisses me with the taste of green apple in his mouth, and asks me if I want to make love once our daughter falls back asleep.

This happiness is unique and profound, and I wouldn't want to risk it for anything in the world.

Out there, the river meets the sea. At the confluence of the two waters, the colours slowly entwine.

After a few kilometres, they become a single colour, a new one.

This aquatic meeting point, where the two waters merge, is called '*les épousailles*,' the nuptials.

The water is cold. I dive like a torpedo toward the underwater forests.

A starfish swims amid the seaweed. I've seen her before; I recognize her: the one with four arms.

Narcisse told me about her.

The river's inhabitants respond as I do when they need oxygen: they change their life's trajectory. They migrate, they move, they hide somewhere else. They try to adapt, if that's still possible. In some places, they won't last more than ten minutes. They escape.

I catch the star and set it in my hand.

To document their panic, scientists tag marine animals.

They put rings on crabs, lobsters, urchins. But starfish refuse to be tracked. They never keep a ring on for more than an hour. They always find a way to escape, even if they have to rip off their arm along with the ring.

I release the star and watch it drift away. The missing fifth arm leaves a void, a hole, an imbalance.

The dismembered star swims, agile with its four arms, managing elegantly with its gap. An amputee, but free.

You won't go in the water, so I tell you about it.

I tell you what it does on your skin. It holds you. New arms. A fresh embrace.

I tell you that I haven't found the blue you're looking for, but that around the green, I've seen yellow, orange, and red.

You nod. It's blue that you're chasing.

'What if the blue you're looking for doesn't exist?'

A tear forms in the corner of your eye. You wipe it away, but I saw it.

I've found a breach, a new way into your heart.

I pass through your shell.

I stay there. This is where you like me.

I slip between your thighs and try to make you laugh.

When I was little, my grandfather's studio had a large collection of paintbrushes. Short bristles, long bristles, coarse, soft. I could spend hours touching them. Imagining the creature they came from.

The horse with the mane cut on an angle, whose forelock is working in the fine arts, or the cow at the slaughterhouse who consoles herself that at least she will have left a trace of herself behind.

One afternoon, I grabbed a long, pliant brush that felt nice in my hand. I wanted to paint with it. My grandfather took out a blank canvas. 'Go ahead. Take your time.'

He said that my brush was sable. At first I thought it was a made-up animal, that he had launched into an Automatiste poem and was weaving new words. But that wasn't it. Sable exists. It's a beautiful animal, one you would want to adopt. It looks a bit like a marten. It's bloodthirsty and can make love for eight hours straight: a record.

I took my time painting that afternoon.

You smile and I kiss you.

I let words fall onto your tongue. I talk to you with my mouth full of saliva. I sketch a map of the underwater colours.

First, there's green, all around.

A viridian, bluish, and transparent green.

Napoleon liked green so much that he covered entire walls of his house with it before dying from the arsenic fumes the colour contained.

The Roman emperor Nero, a despot and a poet, supported the green team in chariot races, collected emeralds, and worshipped leeks.

There are no green threads in Muslim prayer rugs; that way there's no risk of stepping on the Prophet's preferred colour.

'And aside from green?'

In my neck, I feel your joy return.

I feel it under my skin.

I repeat the colour of the depths. 'Red, orange. A bit of yellow, too.'

And then they all disappear. As they came. In the same order.

They say that further offshore, out deeper, it's grey. Only grey, which swallows everything. The grey of sandstone, thick, uniform, intimidating.

Hisaé knocks on my door. She's holding two glasses, as always.

'So? The writing? Any progress?'

'Nope.'

'Well, at least I have gin.'

She's in pyjamas. Blue silk pyjamas. I stand in the doorway and ask her to name the blue of her pyjamas.

'If I get it wrong, are you not going to let me in?'

'If you get it wrong, you have to tell me a love story in Japanese.'

A pause.

'Deal.'

Hisaé looks at the wide legs of her pyjamas.

'Sapphire blue?'

I consider this. Yes, okay.

'Accepted.'

Hisaé comes in, proud and elegant in her sapphire-blue pyjamas.

'But I don't speak Japanese.'

Even dressed in silk, she seems to have stepped out of a boxing ring.

I show her the image of a painting I just found.

A painting from my grandfather's Tachist period, in which a sky blue sits alongside azure. The two blues touch and spread in larger swaths over the canvas, in a luscious brown and sun-orange he created himself.

The painting is called *Petite Anaïs chérie,* Darling Little Anaïs.

It was painted in 1982.

In front of the river.

Hisaé would have guessed it. You can make out the river. You can make out the childhood even more.

The painting frolics, plays in the sand, and has dirty hands.

I was three years old, my mother was carrying my brother in her belly, and we had met my grandfather and his wife for a picnic.

Marcel had a studio on the water's edge.

'Did you know that in French cornflower blue is *bleu barbeau*?'

Alexandre Dumas wrote in *The Count of Monte Cristo* that a handsome young man, 'dressed in a bright blue frock-coat, nankeen trousers, and a white waistcoat,' presented himself before the mayor of Marseille. In the French, the bright blue is described as *bleu barbeau*.

Dumas's *bleu barbeau* evokes the colour of the flower.

Marcel's *bleu barbeau* is the colour of the river and all of the sky, before which he spent his days painting.

My grandfather also collected pebbles made smooth by the salt and drew portraits of them, little travelling pebbles rendered glorious by his brushstrokes.

Marcel clings to his paintbrushes like oars; he's trying not to capsize.

But Marcel's *bleu barbeau* suggests a tipping point. *Petite Anaïs chérie* was his last painting before falling into a long depression. In his next painting and those that would follow, small black marks started to appear in the midst of the blue, separating colours, dividing them. They materialize and grow from one painting to the next, taking up all the space.

My grandfather would be hospitalized a long way from the river, where he found the walls too tall and the minds too small.

He would remain in the shadows for four years.

When he emerged from the dark, Marcel worked with his hands. Dawn till dusk, he built a white sculpture, a survivor, like a breath after nearly drowning. He raised four sails that embrace the wind, ready to flee by water in the event of a tear.

The monumental sculpture has a name like a prayer: *Liberté, liberté chérie*. Liberty, sweet liberty.

It sits alongside the Lachine Canal, which shares its waters with the river.

My grandfather never lost his desire to paint, only his desire to live.

As a little girl, I would go kneel in his shadow sometimes, on the warm floor of his new studio, Rue Amherst. I would make families out of paintbrushes, and sometimes I would make them draw.

Marcel wouldn't look at my drawings much, but he always found them interesting. He never said 'beautiful.' He said 'interesting.'

For my eighth birthday, my grandfather gave me a dollhouse inspired by the family home he had dreamed of under the watchful eye of Paul-Émile Borduas, a professor at the furniture school, the École du Meuble, but that he had never built. I would make a family of Playmobil figures play, sleep, and eat in it, with a grandfather who was an artist.

When I turned ten, he made me an enormous castle for my fourteen guinea pigs. A cage shaped like a house, without bars, a large, two-storey palace, with windows that opened and a spiral staircase.

When I turned fourteen, he gave me Nietzsche's *Thus Spoke Zarathustra*, a reflection on good and evil, in which Zarathustra, the Persian apostle of immorality, invited me to shed my mistakes in the name of life, the only value worth a damn.

On my eighteenth birthday, I climbed a ladder and, arms extended, I flipped through the pile of paintings to choose one, mine, my first painting. My eyes were lined in kohl, my midriff was bare, and I was wearing a pleather miniskirt. I listened to Nirvana on a loop. My grandfather thought I looked like his first wife. The one who left. I didn't know her, I didn't care. I didn't care about much of anything. I learned that from Nietzsche. I chose a painting with a blue background, with pink fireworks and grey above them. It was untitled. Marcel said I could give it any name I like. I left with *Nevermind* under my arm. I walked around the metro with my large-scale Barbeau. I dropped it in the corner of my bedroom. There was no space on the walls, already covered with handsome grunge boys and posters of obscure films.

Hisaé rolls a joint. Her rough fingers scrape the rolling paper and sound like sandpaper.

'Do you still have it? *Nevermind*?'

Yes. When my grandfather died, I hung *Nevermind* in the middle of a wall so bare that I made it into a window, where the blue of the painting blends with the blue of the sky. It sits not far from Marcel Barbeau's last painting, in a dazzling yellow, painted just hours before his death.

Hisaé passes me the joint. I smoke and little twigs stab my lips.

Hisaé leaves thorns on everything she touches.

She takes a shallow bowl out of her bag and places it on my window ledge.

'A gift.'

Hisaé gives me an old ashtray.

I let the ash fall on the brown, still-damp clay.

'Did you find it underwater?'

Hisaé smokes and nods.

Yes. Basque fishermen came from afar, their ships weighted down for smoother sailing. But when they reached the shore, the cod was biting, and they had to offload to make room for the fish. They tossed their bowls, their utensils, and anything they could, overboard, to fill the ship and bring food home to their families across the ocean.

'An old Basque sailor ate from your ashtray three hundred years ago,' she says, laughing.

I take the little clay pot in my hands with new emotion. I empty out my ashes, ashamed to have dirtied it. I clean it with the pad of my thumb.

Underneath, there's the shape of a star, inexpertly engraved. A signature. To say: this is mine; it's my bowl; my wife made it with her own hands, out of love. This is where I eat.

'It's precious.'

'Yes, it's precious.'

It's very warm in the room. Hisaé fills my glass and squeezes a lemon. A few seeds sink to the bottom. Hisaé counts them. One, two, three seeds: 'Death is nigh.'

Her grandmother reads lemons. It's the only language Hisaé learned from her country.

A straggling seed zigzags down my glass.

Four: 'You have a happy home.'

Hisaé is stretched out on my bed; I'm stretched out on the floor. From here I can see the sky.

She doesn't speak Japanese, so she tells me a Japanese love story instead.

The story of Hajime and Shimamoto. He's married with a family. He's happy.

He's reunited with his childhood friend, someone he loved so much before losing her. And from that point on, he loses control.

Their attraction is more absolute and of the interior world than simple physical attraction. *Just as some people have a secret love for rainstorms, earthquakes, or blackouts,* he loves the powerful signals and secrets the opposite sex sends him. Shimamoto inhales Hajime. The force of their attraction is irresistible.

Murakami writes: *The closest comparison might be the power of perfume. Perhaps even the master blender himself can't explain how a fragrance that has a special power is created. Science sure can't explain it. Still, the fact remains that a certain combination of fragrances can captivate the opposite sex like the scent of an animal in heat. One kind of fragrance might attract fifty out of a hundred people. And another scent will attract the other fifty. But there also are scents that only one or two people will find wildly exciting.*

Hajime knows how to recognize this unique odour from very far away. And when he is reunited with Shimamoto, he tells her. He tells her that others may not understand that perfume, but that he does. He understands.

'Hijame,' said Shimamoto, a long time later. 'Do you know any good rivers? A pretty river in a valley, not too big, one that flows fairly swiftly right into the sea?'

Taken by surprise, I looked at her. 'A river?'

She asks him to take her on a trip.

He agrees – he can't say no to her – and leaves his family behind.

Hisaé stops here.

I'm suddenly wide awake. She has stung me without even touching me.

'Why did you tell me that story?'

Hisaé doesn't move. She's as stolid as a walrus in the sun.

'Because it's universal.'

'I'll never leave my family.'

Hisaé smiles.

'Of course not.'

On the window ledge, a ladybug is dying, on its back. Its little brown wings are spread, its legs are flailing. I flip it over with my fingers to count the dots on its back before it dies. Twelve. It seems to weigh so much that it turns back over again to die a little lighter.

I swirl the last swig of gin in my mouth. I have a seed on my tongue and sand between my teeth. I shiver.

'What does one seed mean?'

Hisaé slowly stands.

'It means: Loved.'

She refills our glasses and approaches, looking me in the eyes.

'To your inspiration!'

The *clink* of our glasses echoes; the flame of my candle flickers in my blue room.

Pablo Picasso was twenty years old when he painted one of his first masterpieces. *The Blue Room*. In it, a woman is washing herself in front of her open window. The bed is unmade, a bouquet of multicolour tulips sits on the table. It's morning. There may have been a man in the picture, one who left early that day.

Researchers recently discovered another painting hidden behind *The Blue Room*. Infrared rays detected the portrait of a man. He has an unruly black beard and a beauty mark on the ashen iris of his right eye. He's holding his head in one hand and touching his lips with a thick finger, adorned with three rings. He's thinking. I'm convinced it's you.

I open my eyes and look for you.

The sun is at its zenith.

I've always wanted to look directly at it.

It burns. Hisaé has disappeared.

I have a headache. I drank too much.

A dead ladybug is floating in the puddle at the bottom of my glass.

I open my window and wash my skin in the light of the day, just like Picasso's painting.

I wash my skin as if I were unfolding a precious piece of fabric, the tablecloth for a summer picnic, a veil for a country wedding, a soft towel for a child when they emerge from the sea.

You make my flesh royal.

Japanese people who love each other don't say it. Saying 'I love you' involves extreme tact and belongs in a very intimate and fragile inner space.

恋 (*koi*) means carnal, passionate love, but we hold it in our heart. It isn't written or spoken lightly.

愛 (*ai*) evokes deep, tender love. 'I love you' is most easily said to children. That's good news, I think.

The two qualities of feeling, 恋 and 愛, sometimes combine.

恋愛. It looks like two dancers.

They are placed side by side to show how love evolves, from carnal to tender.

The reverse also exists. 愛恋. A tender love story that turns passionate.

Arranged this way in a story, one love resting on the other, 'I love you' is easier to say.

A man advances along the shore, in the river up to his knees.

He bends over, takes a measurement, and writes something in his little notebook.

He looks like an elongated bird. A tired crane.

I walk toward him because I'm looking for you. It's the only search that interests me. Has he seen the artist?

He stares at me with eyes that are too blue. I prefer black eyes. His lack mystery.

A boat heads toward us, and I look for you on it. The man with the chlorine eyes asks me your name, but I'm keeping you to myself.

His name is Zach. He looks at the waves building and breaking on the shore. He's measuring their effect. The wake of boats creates a series of waves that are eroding the island. They're corrosive.

Before heading out to the next wave, Zach points to the southern tip of the island. He tells me that if he were a painter, that's where he would go.

I head south without asking why.

A few pieces of seaweed are strewn on the shore. Their surface is slimy, preventing them from getting tangled with each other and maintaining their independence.

I take a piece in my hands, run it through my fingers; it becomes my rosary, supports my mantra.

I see you. You're there.

At the tip of the island, the point where you can make out the mainland.

In the distance, there's the silhouette of a bridge.

That's the horizon you're facing, standing in front of your easel.

Narcisse emerges from the water before you. My manubrium cracks when I see you moving in front of your easel. You're drawing her.

Her angular body emerges from the water, glistening. She is foam. She advances, with her back to the sky, facing you, committed to each of her steps, a thousand suns reflected in the drops that cling to her body.

It takes just a second to send me back into my shell. I have this instinctive ability to shut myself in. I become an oyster. I protect myself from you.

I turn on my heel as if I were leaving you.

On Tuesday, November 11, 1890, Claude Monet is sitting at a table in a restaurant waiting for his friend, the artist Gustave Caillebotte. Monet has a drink, grows impatient, and orders some food, as he waits for his guest's supposedly imminent arrival.

But time passes and night falls without the two friends meeting.

Gustave memorably stands up Claude Monet, who will forgive him only upon reading a letter that arrives a few days later.

'Dear Claude, my orchid has been in bloom since this morning, and as the flower only lasts three days and won't bloom again for another year, I can't leave it. My apologies.'

The artist had to seize the fleeting beauty of the present moment.

I prefer dandelions to orchids. They don't demand attention. They risk the alleys and the underbrush. When their lives are done, they grow lighter and fly away. They see the orchids from above. Dandelions are wild and have no regrets.

Sacha knows that on the shores of the St. Lawrence there's a giant lily, the white petals of which unfold only every seven years. Then the flower dies, leaving behind a small shoot on a mission: it will take up the torch and grow giant in turn, seven years later.

Sacha has marked in his agenda the next nine opportunities he will have to see the lily bloom.

According to his projections, he will be one hundred and three years old when he last sees the flower.

In the meantime, he walks the alleys and the underbrush.

Sacha cares as much about dandelions as lilies.

The golden house seems to have moved even closer to the river.

I walk around it in bare feet.

What do we leave behind when our lives take on water?

A small porcelain box forgotten at the top of a cupboard.

I open it. It's filled with baby teeth. All the lost teeth, a mouse's footprints in the snow, collected in exchange for a dollar or two. These maternal moments worthy of a prize, the nights of courage when, heart pounding, I slip my hand under Ama's pillow to make magic, to make her childhood last.

I never would have forgotten them on a shelf. I slip the little box into my pocket; it will help me find my way. Baby teeth as compasses.

I stretch out on the abandoned ground. The exiles took naps under this same sun.

I place my hands on my belly. They are independent, with an intelligence and sensitivity all their own.

They feel wiser than me. Their presence reassures me.

There are several ways to take in the world. We can think about it with our heads, but I find that thinking with our hands works too.

Christian culture sanctified vision as the first among senses. In ancient civilizations, hearing was the primordial sense.

What I want is a civilization of touch.

My hands are rafts on my skin.

I don't need you.

I fall asleep.

The sun at its zenith rouses me. The house trembles. The bells are ringing underwater.

Hisaé swam out this afternoon.

She was looking for submerged quays, but didn't find any.

We're sitting in the little wooded area, smoking.

I'm a smoking oyster.

'Why are you looking for quays?'

Hisaé brightens. I've never seen her body so lively. Her large arms suddenly seem light. She traces lines in the air, sketching her passion for me.

The quays are a hyphen between the wild and the civilized. If Hisaé finds a quay, she finds the footprints of those who walked it.

The footprints of an Irish family on a layover after days at sea, still with a few kilos of hope on their backs, grimy children hidden in the folds of a skirt.

A few pine boards that had become a rest stop for so many migrants, who eat a dry biscuit before starting the great crossing west. People are expecting them there. They still believe it. They talk about it amongst themselves. There will be work. And wide-open spaces to run.

They may return disappointed to the same boards, the same quay, a few years later. It's the quay that knows. It has seen others before them.

When Hisaé finds a quay, she also finds traces of hope and defeat.

The women who waited for fishermen called out to sea. The women who danced with their feet in the water, above the line of their underskirts, because it felt good. The women who, backs broken, held a child with their arms extended to get them used to the waves.

The men who returned, arms filled with cod. The men who didn't return. The men who, legs weakened from loss and pain, delivered their dead to the mainland.

Hisaé stands, getting into it.

'If I find a quay, it definitely has tears soaked into its boards and bits of soles caught in its wood. And who has never dropped something under a quay? That's where I'll find a fortune!'

Hisaé's deep laugh is something to behold.

My shell flakes off a little, the oyster lets in a wisp of air and rays of light.

Hisaé plucks urchin spines from her hands.

Her fingers look worn, older than her. Drops form on her skin. Hisaé tells me that her hands never dry. As if she has become waterproof with time. We lean over the still droplets on her palms. They seem at home.

Hisaé doesn't find a quay. But she finds a mountain of coral offshore.

Coral is my favourite animal, because it can't get away. It lets itself be approached.

Patiently, over centuries, it builds a hard skeleton that anchors it to the ground.

It's a refuge for fish and shellfish.

I've always thought that survival was related to fear, and fear to movement.

Coral, wise and still, proves the opposite.

If we don't destroy it, the old skeleton will outlive us.

The sky turns pink; the tide is rising. Clouds grow puffier. Swollen with our water.

How would you paint where the sky meets the water?

How would you draw the limit, the point of connection – or separation?

I wish you were coral so I would always know where to find you.

My phone rings. It's a call from home. I don't answer. I head out to look for you.

A clatter in my pocket distracts me. I don't throw away the baby teeth; I scatter them one by one behind me. They will show me the way back, in case I go astray.

I am Germaine, I am Simone, I am Pauline.

I tear dogma into confetti that gets caught in the hair.

I have a party in which I undo systems and weave them into lace, in which I grow secrecy like a rare plant in perdition, in which I care for my desire like I care for my sex, my flesh, my heart.

I unbraid the traced lines of my horizons and make them into jump ropes.

I walk toward you. This image will come back to me often, the polaroid of the mystery lover.

If I could have photographed the exact moment when I realized I love you, it would be here, it would be now. You're sitting with your back to me, your shoulders slightly raised, in a state of permanent surprise. Your mica hair is in conversation with the sun.

I hear you faintly singing a song in Spanish.

The moment is both banal and monumental.

Within these few metres, a story is being written. An important story.

I realize my connection to you has gotten away from me. I'm attached to you. Knotted, mired.

I walk in a space in which I don't recognize myself, and, with each step, the previous one is erased along with the life behind it.

I walk toward you, toward only you.

I reach you, I almost touch you. You turn toward me. You stop singing, but you keep the slightly rough, romantic undertones of a Mexican ranch hand about you. The taste of another era, another time, that you don't show and that sleeps inside you.

At your feet are all the colours you're working with. You have put them in shells arranged in a rainbow. It's pretty. You go from grey to white like a musician with his scales; you're looking for harmony. Your canvas has no colour on it yet.

You point to the horizon and the arch of the bridge in the distance.

The view of the mainland reassures you. You're afraid of the void.

And the water is rougher over there. It taunts the immobile iron structure; it cares nothing about its wisdom.

You admire the majestic curves of the bridge and its massive frame, which looks so light. Whoever designed it loved the river. They took the time to glorify the encounter between humans and water, and you're moved by the care they took to create beauty.

You speak with your hand resting on your jaw, like the man hidden behind Picasso's *The Blue Room*. Your finger moves over your chin, your lip, an unconscious gesture that capsizes me. It's the gesture you make when you're thinking.

You're often thinking. Capsized is my new state.

I like being off-balance.

I sit down near you. You brush a few grains of sand from my cheeks.

You ask whether I was crying.

I smile. 'I never cry.'

You rest your hand on my thigh. It bores into me and warms me.

You riddle me with holes.

You tell me people started building bridges when they stopped being afraid of the other.

The unknown is on the other side, of course, but we risk the encounter.

'Civilization began that day. The day when, emerging from the caves that protected them, people built bridges.'

The wind comes up, and you put an incandescent arm around my wax shoulders.

You are both polarities at once; you make me hot and cold.

We usually cross bridges without noticing them.

But you stop to look. And you notice that, despite their enormous pillars, they're fragile and destructible.

And since your pillars are built on the memory of your mother, you tell me about her.

The buzz of the fluorescent lights weaves a web in her head. Despite her armour, she feels her illness chafes everyone she meets.

So she takes off her hospital gown, which smells of clean detergent and a cozy home.

She crosses the hall, and her eyes sweep the doors that open onto all the lives sharpened by scalpels. She doesn't avoid their eyes; she collects their gazes in her pocket like a handful of marbles to lose oneself in if one still wants to get lost.

She goes outside, and trees are what she sees first. They reassure her and seem to clear a path for her. They show her the way.

She weaves her way through the rest of the living; she no longer asks how they do it. She envies them. She continues to love them like a foreign species. She would never be able to learn. Maybe it can't be learned.

She has gone to the end of that land, to the point of suffering. All you can do is come back, she was told, but anyone who says that must be unfamiliar with this place.

She walks among them, trying not to hurt anyone; her armour of darkness is heavy and slows her step.

The bridge is waiting for her over the water like a sway-backed man. She walks onto its iron belly, scratches it like a signature before hauling herself onto its side.

Does she have vertigo?

Staring into the void. The void below, the void of the body too.

The river, wide and vibrant, is waiting for her.

She jumps.

A woman sinks into the St. Lawrence River. The sun pierces the water and accompanies her slow descent. Reds disappear. Yellows, oranges, and greens too. She passes through the grey.

A sliver of light guides her to the river's blue. Where the sandbar ripples. These are the arms your mother dies in.

You're my daughter's age, and you see to it that you'll never be abandoned again.

There are leavings in my wake as well. Does that explain our bond?

In my home, the loving pillars left, and I stayed behind, the tail of the comet of multiple abandonments. I call out 'present' very loudly when asked, to cover for their absences.

I ardently make up for it all, my unshakeable joy slicing through what was left of the darkness.

It's not a mission. It's a definition.

Are our ancestral vertigos in conversation with each other?

Our histories won't let us leave.

I hide away to love you.

Because you hone my vitality, you refine it. Because at your side, I feel chained to the seconds, I inhabit them whole. Because I touch I see I taste I smell for the first time with you. Because you fill me with life. Because I've never felt all this before you.

Your thigh rests against mine. Your heat continues to pierce my body while you build me a century-old house in battens, sprockets, eaves, and skylights. The words in your mouth erect a shelter for me.

You revere the perfection of old buildings, how they fit in with the landscape, but you prefer small dwellings even more, homes you can hold in a hand. You have the soul of a satellite, you dream of lightness. You would live in the patient humility of a village dug into a mountainside; you would live in a Moroccan ksar.

And to think I want you to be immovable coral. I will learn to run to follow you.

You're discreet and talk about yourself only in small bites.

I collect them, store them deep in my pocket in a little box for baby teeth: you like picnics, penknives, trees, live models, and South American poets. You don't like people who leash their dogs or talk too loud. You like notebooks, clotheslines, hand knits, fresh figs, and sailboats. A dark cloud forms when you talk about wealth, and you light up when you tell me about the painters you admire.

You talk about them as if they were your friends. Andrew, Gerhard, Tom. They all painted the wild waves. They stand upright and robust, like you, facing the canvas. It's hard to tell whether they're leaning on it to avoid falling or challenging it to a duel.

You've folded up your easel.

Our words move in our very own ballet.

You like my head. You take it in your hands like a globe, place it on your shoulder.

All your paths have always existed in me, but I had never taken them before.

I want you when you're thinking; your intelligence excites me; I want you to come inside me and fill me with your thoughts.

We stay. We don't go back.

Night falls, and I spread a tablecloth on the ground. Underneath us, the waving, untameable grasses breathe me in. I picked an urchin, and I open it with my hands. I take its belly in my fingers and place it on your saliva-coated tongue that I would like to make my country.

You savour it, and I watch you. I taste it just as much this way.

I roll a cigarette, and you smoke it with me.

The night makes your skin even paler.

I wander along its furrows again, all around your eyes.

Your long black eyelashes give your eyes wings, and the smoke escapes from your mouth. This mouth, like an affront to your restraint. Your lips are the opposite of dark, peonies in August; impetuous, insolent, festive.

You hand me the cigarette, and I put it between my lips so I can touch you right away.

A bit of your saliva remains, and I mix it with mine in a minor victory.

With you, I feel both less alone and more abandoned.

Towering poplars storm the sky. We stretch out on the quay, which has become our witness. Above us, the trees form giant doors we're swallowed up into. The forest is a new city; we wander through Paris, and, at the entrance to Notre-Dame, you take my hand.

You tell me about the gothic churches and their sylvan inspirations: people have always gathered their thoughts in wood, in its whisper. They erected cathedrals in oak groves, the vaults carved with foliage, the columns that line the walls ending abruptly like broken trunks.

They've even imitated the forest's song, the organ inspired by the wind and the bells by the storm.

I tell you about the streets of Isfahan, where I would like to walk with you.

Blue mosaics cover the city walls, their embellishments so detailed that they tell new stories every time you look. In Iran, religious architecture is sensual, even sexual. The domes are rounded like the breasts of a nursing mother, and all around them minarets touch the sky; entire walls are populated with Persian miniatures where couples embrace: men with women, women with women, men with men. We walk at the intersection of profane and sacred art.

Side by side, stretched out on our island quay, we visit cathedrals and mosques.

Being with you is the opposite of being in a new land.

Being with you is my only, my new, my final homecoming.

I'm certain that, if all the social taboos about eroticism were to disappear, what would remain is the experience I sometimes call 'inner nakedness,' when, squeezed onto an island for two, lovers reveal themselves, physically and psychically, a risk we are never permitted to take, that we never want to take, except in a state of desire. Eros is insular.

– Belinda Cannone

We're in the middle of the water, and I undress you. The roof of Notre-Dame and the dome of the Sheikh Lotfollah Mosque protect us, and my bare belly touches yours. The river flows under our bodies and when you penetrate me, I recognize you. I recognize the gentle release of familiar things. I grip your skin; I grab handfuls of your body; you're the distillation of flavours I was searching for. Together we are the essential and only answer.

Your breath and your music blend with the fingers of the trees; love makes sounds that cut through the night. I want to keep you there, forever, your sex buried inside me and seaweed in my mouth.

We are of the same sap. Let's run away.

The island has gone to sleep. I hear laughter, and you hear it too.

It's Narcisse, emerging from the water nearby.

There's a shining circle around her. The river is sending her light signals. She makes us out in the darkness. She shouts, 'It's shining.' As if she were shouting, 'Merry Christmas.'

She paid a nighttime visit to her seaweed, and the water began to shine.

The luciferin sparkles at her feet, like a handful of sugar dropped on the beach. The same glowing molecule lights up the firefly, phytoplankton, and Narcisse, who could make herself a crown with it and take Luciferin as her middle name.

'These are called blue tears in the Caspian Sea.'

We walk along the shore together.

Under our feet is the outline of new constellations. The sky and the ground inverted.

Narcisse's heavy braid dances between her jutting shoulder blades. I want to carve a brush from it for you.

Narcisse has retained a childlike gait, her step both grounded and joyful.

She seems to have come straight out of a Makhmalbaf film. Her tanned skin has a 35-mm grain.

The little heroines of Iranian films casually carry the world on their shoulders. They hang juicy cherries from their ears, stain their lips with grenadine, and swing their hips in overalls. They challenge censorship with moments of bewildering yet blameless sensuality.

What dictatorship can criticize a girl for biting into a lemon? What would be the reason for banning this scene, even though it's filled with saliva, daring, and desire? Iranian filmmakers have found ways to foil the forbidden. They have found a place where their freedom can survive.

By putting sunny children on the screen, engaged in simple quests.

Children with swagger who want something: to buy a goldfish, to find a friend's home, to go to a baseball game.

Narcisse wants to be reunited with Jonas. He captured his iceberg. He's towing it to sea, hitched to his boat, proud of his catch. He'll be back soon. Jonas is a hero.

I wake up in your arms on the deserted shore.

I head under the branches of the big poplar and pee on the fish bones of Notre-Dame.

I watch you from here. You're sleeping with your knees tucked toward your chest, your long arms open toward my absence. Your hair moves in the wind, and everything else is still. I don't understand the place you already occupy in me. I didn't need you. You quickly became my resonance chamber. My explanation.

You wake up.

I invite you into the water.

At this point, you grow serious again.

To hold on to you, I have to grab you by the eyes.

You have a dark spot in the ashen iris of your right eye.

I've told you this before. You had never noticed it.

I've found my full stop, and I cling to it so I don't fall, but it's too late and I know it.

Milan Kundera writes that vertigo is an encounter with our own fragility.

I feel like I'm walking on the border of you.

I invite you in again. I want to touch the water with you.

You come. It's a declaration of love.

We walk into the water, side by side. The cold climbs up our thighs, shivers rush to your neck like a storm.

We let the tide rise inside us.

Hisaé tells me that my phone rang three times that morning. She can hear it through the wall.

It's the long-term care home.

The home where Janine lives, my almost-grandmother, the one who took my mother in when she was little.

The voice on the other end of the line is worn out from constantly dispensing reassurance: Janine is fine. But she had some heart trouble yesterday. 'A bit of a twinge.' It could happen again.

The worn-out voice doesn't sound too worried, but I feel like she's suggesting I come.

If I leave the island, I leave you. I can't.

Sacha is on his way to the market with Ama on his shoulders. He's talking to me full screen; I see his gentle face framed by my daughter's long legs. Ama has her Frida socks on, pulled up to her bruised knees, the knees of a child who plays. Her father's large hand is holding her thigh, and I know he's protecting her from all the falls that lie in her future. I wanted to ask him to go watch over Janine's heart, but I can't. I've always rejected guilt as a toxic burden that needs to be jettisoned. But this morning, seeing this happiness, it suffocates me, and even my tongue feels guilty. I have a hard time forming words.

'Maman?'

Ama saves me yet again.

She is silhouetted against the sky. The new day makes a little beret of sun for her.

She tells me that the cat is pregnant: she has a big belly and the tips of little breasts poke out through her fur.

'Pet her.'

I manage to get that out. Just that. I smile and hang up.

I stay alone in my blue room, which suddenly feels foreign.

The river's voice is making noise.

Hisaé comes in without knocking.

'Take him with you.'

We will make only one trip. A return trip, like a boomerang, like paddleball, like Canada geese in the spring, all things that return. We will be clandestine.

You accept my proposal. As if for marriage. You say you will go with me.

I don't know what will be left of us there. Our love is an islander. It doesn't mix with the earth. Our love is maritime, and the city could just dry us up.

Maybe it would be simpler.
If the trip could be our undoing.
If urbanity could split us apart.

You drive. The road gives me a chance to settle into the details of your profile; I can look at you without interruption. I ease into this space that you can't see. I follow the trace of the tiny waves under your ear. The ripples of your skin. The road toward a tiny oasis, the receptacle for your scent. I don't need a fortified city; this is where I curl up, huddled in the hollow of your neck, protected from everything, at last.

We reach the city. It hits me like a death-metal party in space. Everything is compact and concentrated, a vibrant density contained in an astronaut's suit.

The feeling I have is both terrifying and magnificent. I moult. I change my chemical nature. My new skin is more porous. On the street, others pass through me. They slip into my body, vent into me, penetrate me, and threaten to break me into a thousand shards.

Their faces and their gaits fascinate me; I want to know all of them.

Their vitality moves me; I feel spread wide, like I'm made of open doors, and they make themselves at home inside me.

It's you. It's us. Our coming together is what's doing this to me. It makes me extraordinarily present to the world, permeable to the lives I meet. I become the resonance chamber of all that exists.

You make me much too expansive.

We've arrived. We stop right in front of the door, in the shade of the tall ash.

It's a no-parking zone.

You're a good person; you follow the rules.

I tell you I always park here, but to do as you like.

I brought shells for Janine. I put them in my bag.

On top of the bottle opener, the lemon, the underwear, the crumbs of rolling tobacco at the bottom, the chocolate, the pens, the pair of socks, the three lighters I can never find, the red nail polish, and a few dog-eared books. You smile when you see me shoving things around with a firm hand. This is the only place I try to contain my life in a confined space.

We're on a road that's too busy for an embrace.

We don't know each other here, not like this.

You fidget a bit, you talk about real things, and you fill the void that's settling in between us; you lead us into the banal, as if that could protect us, as if we have the right to exist here. I kiss you anyway. I kiss you in the city. I kiss you on a busy street. It's a quick kiss, a kiss that makes a statement, that says 'I can love you here too.' I take that risk.

I enter the beige lobby of the large beige building with an air of nobility. As if a long train of springtime were floating behind me.

I smile at the tired attendant who is doing a crossword puzzle at reception.

I've come to see Janine. How's she doing?

But the only thing the attendant knows about my great-aunt is her room number, which she has taken pains to memorize.

I want to take a bit of this love that has stripped me of my shell and made me softer; I want to share it with the tired attendant who hands me the log with the chicken scratch of all the other tired hands. All the people who are worn down. All they need is just a bit of you for them to shed their skin.

I take the elevator up to the sixth floor with a man in pyjamas in a wheelchair. He stares at the numbers on the screen as they light up one by one. One, two, three, four. Like a reverse countdown that brings him back to the solitude of his room. He has big, pink wool socks that he hikes up to cover his calves. His hands are large, his palms broad, and his fingers slender. He has touched cheeks with the backs of those hands, maybe wiped away tears. He has held breasts in them, encircled buttocks. He has squeezed lemons and sorted pennies with those large hands that are pulling up his socks.

Fifth floor. He has held women against him, hands resting just below their shoulder blades, as they dance. *Parlez-moi d'amour, redites-moi des choses tendres. Speak to me of love, tell me tender things again.* He has put his hands to his forehead to hide his sobs, and he has broken a jaw or perhaps split a temple, then petted his cat.

Sixth floor. I get out. The old man and his hands continue their ascent without me. I'm going to see Janine.

She isn't expecting me. Janine is never expecting anything but surprises. Her memory is gone and has been replaced by relaxed expectations. She takes things as they come, and today, what comes is me. Me, in love.

I find her sitting in her armchair, a package of chocolate cookies she has started on beside her, Charles Aznavour on the radio, as she hums along, the last bastion of her memories.

'He says such nice words!' she says, admiring.

She lights up when I walk in; she doesn't quite know who I am, but she knows, she feels, that I love her and she loves me back. There's no time left for detours when you're ninety-four. You love me, I love you. The path is mapped out.

Janine's cheeks are rosy. I'm reassured to see her this way. She doesn't seem frail or sick. The pictures pinned to the wall bring me back to my constellation. To my daughter, skinned knees, her mouth smeared with ice cream.

To my man, with his cat eyes, an arm around my waist as if I were a rocket, ready for liftoff.

I turn my back on them.

I've brought coloured marshmallows. I make it my mission to get Janine walking so her legs don't get rusty. I ask whether I'm putting her life at risk, but the young man who bathes her, talks to her, cares for her, changes her, and listens to her, the young man who now knows her better than anyone gives me the green light and a smile. He's twenty years old, and he was born 3,096 kilometres away from here.

I invite Janine into the garden.

Gripping her walker, she greets the neighbours. We move from one solitude to the next, the room doors open onto the final vanities of a life.

The walls of the elderly are like a beach at low tide, covered with surviving remains.

A straw hat, a slingshot, a birthday garland, a dried carnation.

An object for a story, an encounter, a love, or a celebration, the map of an unsteady memory.

In the end, we decide to start with the mauve marshmallow during the countdown trip in the elevator, because 'mauve marshmallow' rhymes in French. *Mauve guimauve.*

We swim against the slow noon current in the cafeteria and open the door to the outside. The small garden awaits us, with its wooden bench, its overcast sky, and its light birds. Dandelions push up through the ground, ever valiant. It's as if they want to hear what we're going to say. They're the only ones who can.

I believe in secrets. I like to have something that doesn't crumble. Things that belong only to us are few and far between.

I bite into the mauve marshmallow and give Janine the other half.

With the tip of her shaped nail, she sections out a crumb and offers it to the birds. A sparrow hops about and pecks at the sugary treat.

Janine greets him.

'That's Georges. He's always here. He likes me.'

Janine swallows the sweet with a delighted 'mmmm.' She loves her food.

Perched on his branch, the bird tries to unstick his beak.

'Is it good, Georges?'

I need to talk to someone too.

In Janine's little garden, I unwrap my secret like a sweet. I can share anything with her. I offer her a fragile piece of me, a secret on the flip side of shame.

Janine finishes off her marshmallow while I try to find my words. It's strange trying to find your words for someone who will immediately forget them.

'Can I have a marshmallow?'

Janine's mouth is mauve, but she has forgotten that she just swallowed.

While her slender, freshly manicured fingers run over her next mouthful, I tell her I'm in love.

She exclaims that this is good news.

'Is it possible to love more than one person at the same time?'

She bites into the green marshmallow.

'It tastes like apple!'

Janine licks her fingers, looks at me, tells me I'm beautiful, that life is beautiful too, asks me what we're doing here, tells me again that I'm beautiful, asks me where we are now, when we're going in, and tells me that loves come by the dozen, sometimes by the hundred. It depends on the person. That we can love someone completely. That we can then love someone else completely. She adds that it's like marshmallows.

And after a time, during which I make little loops of all the wrinkles on her face, applying myself to imagining them tied into delicate bouquets that could be a centrepiece for a table at a wedding, like a pretty omen, after a time, Janine tells me that we can get bogged down in strange rules.

The heart can too. Even more so the heart.

I seize this fragile perch to ask her how hers is, how her heart is.

She looks at me as if I were asking the only question that matters.

At that very moment, I sense in her eyes all the smiles she has allowed to bloom in her, ever since she was a little girl. There are thousands of them. The surplus smiles stream from her eyes.

Pain and joy are porous to each other as death approaches. It's hard not to miss past happiness.

But Janine tells me her heart is light; she can't complain.

The heart of the blue whale weighs 180 kilos and beats only twice a minute.

'Incredible, isn't it?'

So I tell her your name. An exchange of wonders. I can't say your name to anyone else, so I say your name, so lovely that it unlaces on my tongue and crumbles on my lips, a breaking wave like an offering, from one age to another, one woman to another. This is the name of the one I love.

She repeats it, loudly. Like she's calling to you. It's as if she loves you too.

'Did you know that Orpheus turned around when Eurydice said his name?'

Janine, her mouth full, eyes on Georges, who is finishing his mouthful of marshmallow, tells me the story of the greatest myth of love.

'Eurydice is trapped in the underworld, far from Orpheus, her great love. He loves her enough to come find her, but to save them, he must absolutely not turn around. She must follow him and, without looking, he must show her the path to their salvation. If he looks back at her, for her voice, for her eyes, for her body, he will lose her forever.

'Eurydice follows quietly in Orpheus's footsteps; they're almost on the other side, where they can love each other. It's all pretty simple, but … '

Janine looks at me now, her eyes magnified by the thick lenses of her glasses. A small white line forms a half-moon above her iris, the beginning of an eclipse.

' … But … Eurydice calls out to Orpheus. She wants to see his face, she wants their scents to mix and their pace to be in step … Eurydice calls out his name: *Orpheus!*

'Ahead of her, he resists his beloved for a while, but his name spoken in the voice of the one he loves, the new existence she has given him, the way she has of bringing him into the world … He turns. They look at each other. They have time to love each other face to face for one second, before she disappears forever.'

I suddenly regret having said your name.

I don't know whether I would survive your disappearance.

I object; the fall seems brutal, severe, unjustified.

Janine disagrees. She stands elegantly, places her hands on her walker.

'No. Eurydice calls out to Orpheus because they're connected. And that's why he turns back.

'Because he's human. And we humans are capable of something astonishing: love.

'Shall we go in now?'

We go back up to her room. Her light heart is tired. She, too, had time to love, much more time than me. She survived. I place the clam shell on the window ledge. It gleams. To determine its age, you count the grooves on its shell, like you would count the rings on a tree.

This one is a hundred years old. Between the jars of Nivea cream and the boxes of chocolate, the nacre of an ancestor reflects the downtown sky.

The drawing of a hippocampus hangs on the wall. Ama learned that it was responsible for memory in the human brain. She carefully pinned it over Janine's bed, hoping it will return.

' … I'm tired. Is that my boat?'

'Yes, that's your boat, Janine. Do you want to lie down?'

'Oh, yes.'

The sun beats a path with her to her bed. I want to draw the curtains, but in a little voice overtaken by sleepiness, Janine says not to. She says, 'Leave the light on.'

I leave the light on.

I take her hands and help her to bed. She protests vociferously. That reassures me.

'You're hurting me.'

'I'm sorry.'

She has almost no skin left. Everything she touches, she touches with her veins. We are of the same blood, covered with a thousand lagoons that become oceans as we age.

That day, she lies down on her bed, her boat. She finds it comfortable and beautiful.

She likes the colour of her blankets, the green and the pink, and asks me to tuck her in. She tells me she's going to die. I stroke her hair. I hide behind words and tell her that we're all going to die, but not just yet. She smiles at me, she tells me I'm beautiful and that life is too, she closes her eyes and says, 'Allons-y gaiement.' Let's go merrily.

I let her have the last word.

But as I leave, I whisper her name, 'Janine.' Just loud enough to hold on to her a little. To pin her identity to her, remind her that her grandeur cracks sealed windows. Her name like the embrace I can no longer offer her because she has no more skin and everything hurts her. Her name to restore her to when she was forty, to pleasure and to fanning the flames.

I leave on tiptoe, my springtime train wrapped around my neck so I don't trip on it.

Moving upstream in the long corridor, I read the names of solitary bodies, I sail through their immobile archipelago. Written by hand in little identical frames, stuck to the edge of each door: Nino Fartelli, Mireille Daoust, Auguste Baptiste.

I say them out loud. I call all the Orpheuses before it's too late.

Love, love, love, I tell them, as long as there's still time.

And in the light of the day, they turn toward me.

Outside, it's even more summer than before, because you are waiting for me.

The car is parked in the no-parking spot; you're sitting on the curb, your legs flung into the street. You're an exclamation point, and I don't know you like this. Your presence is loud, and I see only you.

I call you by name.

You lift your head from your book to bore your seductive eyes into mine, which are seduced.

I ask you to go for a walk through the city streets. Because I don't know whether we will ever be able to again. I want to hold your hand in the midst of nine billion people, but you don't want to. The city is humid and festive, and I walk two steps away from you.

You're not my man, and I'm not your woman. The city makes the ground split beneath our feet, creates a deep trench between us, reminds us that we are ephemeral.

We walk along, watching for looks, reining in our impulses with a bit. I want your hand on me and your body on me; I want to claim the right to be yours.

I let you take root. I feel it: you take my soil with you when you leave.

You inhabit me, bombard me, colonize me.

I walk through these unfamiliar streets with you. They're filled with the steps of others, and I want only ours. I want to crush everything in our path.

I want to erase the paths already created and be woven only to you; I want to tear up old ties, have them fall like dead ropes, knots undone, unbound forever.

I advance for you, I feel for you, I gather for you, I listen for you, I'm in this world for you. Tied to you, I am free.

I experience you like a trampoline. You propel me toward my essence because it interests you. You're thirsty, and I want to give it to you. I want you to fill yourself with it, I want you to inhale me down to the bone.

Wait up. I cross the invisible trench, slip my hand under your shirt. I touch your white back and pierce your skin in turn. I don't care what the people looking at us think.

I'm not dependent. I'm fiercely attached to all your landscapes.

I choose you; I have but one life.

Through the open windows, a party. Conversations and bursts of laughter pour into the street. Inside, the cold sharp blue lighting contrasts with the weight of the air.

Bodies sway in time with the summer, music moves through their tissues, and everyone embraces.

We crash the party. We scrutinize faces, making sure we are anonymous.

You want to leave; you never park in a no-parking zone.

Drink. I pour a smoky scotch down your throat.

Dance. I learned to desire too late, but now I'm wise, and I'm making up for lost time. I wield my desire, and it makes me stronger. Wanting you is my most beautiful living posture.

I delight in you. Let's dance.

I take your hand, and our lifelines flow together. A passage opens up before us like a biblical sea. We move to the middle of the living room, where other bodies rejoice alone together. We're in a land where people dance alone, as if demanding their freedom.

I'm alone with you now. I give you my movement, I dovetail with yours; I wrap around your hips and your breath.

We're in perfect equilibrium between freedom and attachment, equal in love and eroticism.

Your head on my shoulder, your face in my neck. Your lower belly against my lower belly. We dance in each other in the middle of the world, sovereign and liquefied.

We sleep in each other's arms in your car.

Dawn breaks over the city; soon we will get back on the road.

You tell me without looking at me that you need more hues. You'll stop at your place to pick up a tube of indigo.

I don't want to.

There was a tacit agreement, a silent wish: we won't get close to our regular lives.

I don't want to be near the people who love you. I don't want my air to encounter your wife's. I don't want to know the neighbourhood or street where you live. I want to believe we exist in two parallel worlds, where I'm not taking anything from her.

I know it's a lie.

I know that what I have with you I've stolen from my partner, I've snatched from my daughter.

But I give it to myself, to me.

You close the car door behind you, and you cross the street to your life.

There's a stroller on the balcony, a ball in front of the door.

A man's bike, yours, leans against a woman's. With your foot, you lift the kickstand that was left down. With just this gesture, I see you in love. Tender, undoubtedly attentive. My body stiffens.

I picture her as magnificent as you.

I look away.

I think about Sacha's shoulders, ice picks I could use to climb Everest. I think of Ama's cheeks, rafts of cotton I can sink into.

Ama who climbs my legs like a koala, a bouquet of lilacs on the table, the cat purring in the living room, the notes from a violin that make the mirror vibrate, windows open onto a rainy day, the squeak of swings, and the voices of children outdoors – gentle, simple joy.

If you didn't come back, I would understand.

But you come back. And you smile when you open the door.

You found the colour you were looking for, and the colour returns to my face.

You take a breath that you seem to have been holding.

You've chosen yourself, too, and it hurts.

We've crossed the line.

We're committing no fault. We're walking through a world of secrets that burn, but it's worth it.

I get out for a moment to leave a shell on the curb. Just in front of the steps to your house. From a soft-shell clam. As delicate as a fine jewel.

An offering.

My way of saying I'm not stealing you. I'm celebrating you.

And what more can we hope for those we love than to be celebrated?

The river is beautiful. I've missed it.

The ripple of the waves and a thin line of foam that dances on them make me want to write. *Tributary, tideland, sandbar*: so many pretty words that roll and break and ice over in the mouth. They say so much, but we read them so little.

In his desire to write the ocean, Baudelaire braved his fears and boarded a massive ship on its way to Calcutta. But, gripped by vertigo, terrified of the magnitude of the story, he was brought back to land. And, finally, in front of the Seine he writes: *Homme libre, toujours tu chériras la mer* – Free man, you will always cherish the sea. The river is where he found his voice.

The way the water wraps around or contains a country influences its writing.

In French literature, the sea is an escape.

In English literature, it's a prison.

Here, we sing the praises of the river's nourishing waters, the jugular of our land.

In foggy geopoetics, nineteenth-century writing drinks from its source.

After sailing the river for the first time, Jacques Cartier named it on August 10, St. Lawrence Day: *a very beautiful and large bay full of islands and fine entry points.*

The river inspires many stories, but with time its story blurs. And when the stories vanish, all they tell of vanishes along with them.

Clo is sitting on the hull of the boat; he's looking out at the water.

I wave to him.

We climb aboard. He asks us for news of the city as he always does, not really wanting to know. Clo doesn't care about the city.

He casts off. The motor covers the silence that he tried to fill.

The surface of the water cleaves as we pass; we open it up, slice through it roughly, and it quickly returns to such calm. I'm drawn into the motion of its oily back.

I absorb everything. I'm filled with the world and emptied of myself.

Philosophers call 'oceanic feeling' the sense of eternity like the feeling provoked by the image of the sea and the endless movement of the waves. The moment the ego dissolves, and we're no longer *before* the world but one with it.

You're sitting at the bow. You're looking into the distance, toward the bridge. You've turned up the collar on your jacket. I'm searching under your coat for the grain of your skin.

I suddenly feel both inside you and on the other side of the world.

I exist all around myself. You swallowed my core.

You are my new story.

You are my oceanic feeling.

Yvonne is waiting for us on the shore. She's been crying. You can tell from her cheeks.

They're puffy with salt.

Clo, at her side, has also been crying. Before, after, or at the same time. They're connected by underground pathways.

Yvonne holds out her hand to help me out of the boat, which Clo ties off to the unsteady quay.

'Narcisse hasn't come back.'

A cloak made of you wraps around me and protects me.

Instinctively you draw closer to me. Worn out from tragedy, primed for horror, you pull me behind your shield.

Narcisse stayed underwater. She didn't come back up from her last dive.

You stagger, and I stagger with you.

The water is choppy.

They searched for her everywhere.

I think about Hisaé's quays. About their memory.

The quays that support us will forever hold in their splinters the eternal memory of a drowning.

They call off the search.

They leave on noisy coast-guard boats. A laugh rises from one of the boats and falls like debris on the water. They don't know Narcisse.

My feet scrape the sand; they sink into it. I would like to disappear a little. It's hard to stay alive with death in your face. It's a big responsibility.

Hisaé passes me the joint and plucks the invisible spines she always has in her hands.

Irène, Clo's granddaughter, plants seaweed as a flag on her sand-castle.

And you escape into painting.

You strain, clinging to your easel, staring at the river that taunts you.

The thief. Its waves come in up to my feet, making lakes where I'm digging.

I stand. I snatch shells from the high-water mark, add a roof of blue mussels to Irène's castle.

I stop looking at the river. I refuse to turn my attention to it, as if I were punishing it.

The child is crouched before the pile of sand she's building with her still chubby hands. Her red hair grows toward the sun, creating a tiara of fire.

'Did you know there's a sand island?'

I didn't know.

Irène is stroking her castle's skin.

'It's on maps of the river, but no one can find it anymore. It was swallowed up by the water.'

' … That can happen … '

'Did you know that wild horses lived on it?'

It's a true story, the little girl says, staring at me with eyes as red as her hair.

'The sand wore down their teeth, and they couldn't eat anymore. They were starving, and they came to drink water from the river before they died.'

Irène sticks her hands in the water, making them dance like palm trees. The grains of sand that cling to her skin flow in a wavy trajectory that she watches until the end.

'The sand covered the bodies of the dead horses and made round dunes on the beaches, and then pretty little migratory birds set down there. They travelled from one end of the sky to the other, carrying their nests on their backs, like a hat.'

The child gathers curly Irish moss, placing it on the roof of her castle.

'The birds put their nests made of twigs on the lifeless bodies of horses and came to lay their eggs in the warmth of the sand.'

Irène's little finger swipes the tear from my cheek and brings it to her mouth.

She furrows her brow. If I were a bird, I would leave my eggs on it.

'Your tears aren't salty?'

I shrug.

The child looks at the river. The child looks at me and smiles.

Cold rain suddenly lets itself in; this is its home.

You abandon your latest canvas to it. You walk away.

The deserted colours fade, while your easel stands alone in the heavy winds – as strange and touching as one of Jean-Jacques Sempé's little cartoon characters.

At the foot of the lighthouse, Yvonne gathers little broken skeletons by the handful. A cloud of terns slammed into the light in the night.

Old Zach refuses to accept the disappearance and is getting ready to go back out on the water. He wants to fish for an explanation.

I hop aboard.

Zach says nothing. He puts up my hood and starts the boat.

It's raining.

Zach knows how to read the river and easily avoids the crying rocks, smooth boulders that point their wet heads toward the surface of the water, cracking the hull of illiterate boats.

You watch me go.

I turn toward the open water before you grow too small.

I prefer not to see you disappear.

'It's a broken heart.'

Zach rarely speaks. In his mouth, the words *broken* and *heart* are revelations. I hear them as if for the first time. This is the fate we should always reserve for words. Rebaptizing them, every time.

You have told me that to paint a wave you need to see it as an apparition. Seeing the world through a child's eyes to write it properly, to paint it properly.

To experience it like it's new.

The silence after the noise of the motor feels like a gunshot.

'It's a broken heart.'

Narcisse lost Jonas; he was crushed under his quarry. The captive iceberg melted, broke apart, and then collapsed. Its waters won't make it to the Canary Islands; its waters will remain wild. Jonas died under their weight.

They already searched the river, its seaweed forests, and its reefs. They found nothing.

We head toward the nets the fishermen cast into the water.

And Narcisse was a strong swimmer.

Zach plunges his withered arms into the darkness, grabs onto the cold, slippery ropes and yanks, but nothing moves, nothing comes up.

The net is too heavy.

'Give me a hand.'

I'm eight years old, and I'm in a bathing suit standing on the high diving board. Suddenly, I'm very afraid of the water. I don't want to dive. I don't want to find Narcisse's body swollen from the water, her eyes made glossy by the depths, her earlobes nibbled by crabs.

I'm frozen in place.

The water quivers. The rain gets heavier; a storm forms in the sky.

The bells ring underwater.

Zach looks at me. 'Do you hear them too?'

I grip the heavy ropes with outstretched arms.

Our bodies lean out toward them. We pull, and at the other end something pulls back.

I resist. My hands are bleeding.

Finally, the net abruptly gives.

Zach falls on me, sending us both to the bottom of the boat.

The catch got away.

The net full of holes covers us and warms us.

It's come from a long way away.

There are bits of seaweed in its oxbows. Hundreds of little pieces of confetti, constellations of kelp hearts, scattered like a party between the tight links of silk threads.

I'm soaked down to my bones. I know you'll be able to warm me.

The waves lick at the side of the golden house, where I find you.

You open your arms to me.

I want to sleep here, with you.

You want to throw up walls, but you're crying.

Never stop. Our connection takes the same path as your tears.

I lick your face clean. You taste like damp earth and royal kombu. I wrap around your shoreline. At the base of your neck, there's a bump, a mountain, the site of buried treasure. In it, I kiss the weight of your history. I suck on your past life. I make your secrets quiver with my fingertips.

I know that your secrets have created your process: your shoulders propel you, your beautiful full head beats a straight path; you pretend you can't see as you move forward without looking back.

I like the wounds buried in your back. I like everything about you.

One day I will belong to your shoulders as well.

I will be part of your blind spot.

I take your sex in my mouth. It stiffens a little under my tongue. I like to hear the song of your breath as you grow hard.

Your sighs reverberate inside me, and I want to understand their precise language.

I make myself a necklace from your breaths strung together.

I don't want them to ever dissipate; I want to collect them, decode them to slip into my pocket the almanac of all that sleeps inside you.

I want to become all your echoes.

You tell me you're going to come. I like this animal courtesy, this bestial elegance.

I drink you in so you will stay inside me. Your sex leaves a groove on my lip. A sign that you were there, that my tongue runs over to remember your pleasure.

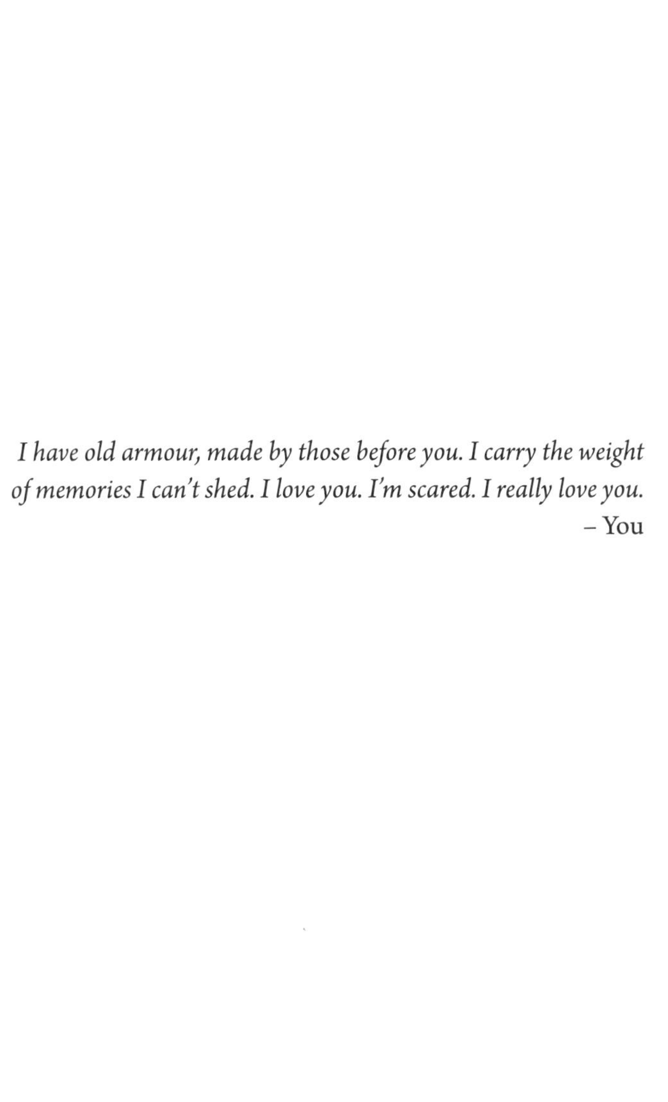

I have old armour, made by those before you. I carry the weight of memories I can't shed. I love you. I'm scared. I really love you.

– You

My back against your torso, your head against mine, we are double parentheses opening onto the night.

Our golden house nods its head in the strong winds. Bound to each other, we run the risk of falling with it. We tame the naked voice of our fears. The rest of the world evaporates in salty water on our sticky skin.

'If you could choose any other life, what would it be?'

You don't hesitate.

You would be the director of the Kyoto National Museum.

You would be the conductor of its major collections, the colour chart of its discourse.

I can picture you perfectly in the refined space of a Japanese museum, your neck stretched toward fine frescos, your back liberated.

You know all the rooms by heart, and you have your favourites, no doubt the narrowest, where you protect a priceless painting from eyes. A Richter, in which the flames of two candles flicker side by side, to the same rhythm, two solitary dancers swaying in the dark. Like us.

You sit down alone in front of the painting, and you warm yourself from it for a while.

You savour each morsel of warmth in the pit of your stomach.

'What about you?'

A beat.

I would grow lemons in a citrus orchard. In Iran.

I would wear a cotton skirt and a blue kerchief in my hair.

'Which blue?'

'Yours. You'll have found it by then.'

I love all the seasons of my trees. I watch over their blossoms, their flowers blooming. Harvest is the most beautiful time, and the hardest.

From winter to spring, the twist of my hand becomes mechanical, and I try to preserve the excitement. I strive to keep the freshness of the first glance.

I pick only the fruit; I don't harm its skin or its leaves or its delicate stem. I am the sower of lemons on arid land, and the nape of my neck burns in the sun.

Silence.

We'll be a long way from each other.

But would we have met?

Yes, we would have met.

We won't be far from each other then.

The significance of an encounter isn't measured in how long it lasts, but in the mark that it leaves.

Through the window, the Pleiades are twinkling. They're the only things the black clouds let through. Seven little stars, clumped together, in asylum.

The daughters of a Titan and an Oceanid, the sisters were too free: Zeus turned them into a constellation to avoid losing them.

That night, they invite me to join them.

The water has risen; the river is eating away at the golden house, and you're not there anymore. I reach land as our kingdom crumbles.

It's dark outside, the wind is blowing on the river, which spews its life force onto what is left of its shores.

At this very moment, your absence grips me from the inside, like taking possession, like colonizing, like desecrating. Your absence becomes what I am made of, my very substance. I am your clearcut.

I walk toward the shore. I no longer fear death.

The river is unleashed; its roar kisses the sky.

The ocean's belly empties onto me. I trample its entrails; I'm searching for you.

It creaks and it scratches under my bare feet. I find a four-armed starfish. It's alive. I stroke its limbs. I kiss the empty space, its missing arm, torn off – the price of its freedom.

I throw the star and its courage out into the water, where it can try to survive. As I walk, I step on another, then another still: the river is spitting back its wild stars, its untamed ones. They are strewn everywhere, dismembered starfish, washed up on the beach, suffocating in chorus. Their final breaths blend with mine; I pick them up by the handful, throw them back into the black water with everything I've got, which just spews them back up more forcefully.

And I see you. You're there, afraid. You bend and you gather and you bend and you gather and you come toward me without seeing me.

The light from the lighthouse sweeps our bodies that are standing face to face. You hold a handful of ringed legs, a thousand solitary arms, a thousand torn-off arms that rest in the palm of your hand. I hold in mine all their other halves.

We are two parts of the same story.

When I dive, you dive too. This time, you come with me.

We don't hold hands. We don't need to; we hold each other all over without even touching.

We dive into the black water because it's the end, and that's what you do with the end; you grab it by the scruff and ask it for a dance or a suicide.

The rain intensifies, and the river's surface splatters under the torpedoes.

Floating around us are the empty shells rejected by the crabs for being too small.

They turn in an orbit, left behind like abandoned homes, little satellites for our lost bodies.

The murmur of the drowned whispers the rest of a story interrupted; voices are reawakened missiles. The shouts of Norwegian sailors, the wails of a Scottish baby, the pleas of a captain. We can't see anything now; we touch our relics with our fingertips. A rocking chair, a dance floor, a quay with no moorings, an easel without you. We read our sediment.

It's grey down here.

Are we dying?

A burst of Narcisse's laughter breaks through in the middle of the storm. It rips through the mesh of nets and frees the fish; her child-like voice whistles in Persian.

We are there. Where the river touches the sea. It's blue.

There's an open oyster. There are shards of an English porcelain cup. There's a Japanese cherry tree in bloom, and a thousand lemon pips turning in a circle.

And you open your mouth at the meeting of waters, to swallow the blue of *les épousailles* – the nuptials, a nascent, unexplored blue. You feed on it like a promise.

We resurface together. Our eyes are bigger than before. In the sandbar, we swim in a flooded field. The river is our home, and it makes us grow gills. A jellyfish glows and leads the way. Like her, we are immortal.

Irène is flying a kite on the beach, holding it with her body outstretched, and she is carried on the current of the winds.

She keeps her hand tight around the strings that pull her to the sky: by extension, she gains a wider perspective.

In Japan, there are kites shaped like fish. On special occasions, for good luck, the sky fills with thousands of flying fish. They say they are an extension of the heart.

There is a story of a young samurai who had disobeyed the emperor and was exiled to a desert island with his only son. To break out of their isolation, he made a kite that they took turns tying themselves to. Days when one of them needed some air, the other held the strings firmly and sent them up into the sky.

That is how they survived.

Standing on the quay, I'm the one left behind. The one who watches you go.

I know this is where we leave each other.

We're not meant for land.

We're water fauna.

This time I watch you grow smaller.

Even invisible, you fill me up.

I will never be alone again.

Hisaé wants to take me with her. Her back is broad enough to carry the weight of my sorrow.

But I don't move. I run aground here. I rub my palms on the planks of the quay to give me splinters; I want all the memories from its sodden wood under my skin.

I watch them leave one by one. Zach, Clo, Yvonne. They surrender, leave the island to be swallowed up without them. Irène stations herself at my side. She's lucky; to live in the water she just needs to add an 's' to the start of her name and drop the 'e' at the end: siren.

She tells me not to cry; they're coming. I had almost forgotten about them. My daughter and her father.

Only a strip of sand remains of the island, where I wait for Ama. My man is walking at the water's edge. Nothing about him is familiar. My body is watertight.

My sadness is cruel.

I can't see its horizon.

It has no threshold.

I sink into it.

My name is sadness.

Ama emerges from the river, little fins on her feet, her body on vacation.

She joins me on the shore.

She is only six years old, but she walks as if she has known the ground far longer. She swims the same way. She shares an alphabet with the elements.

Her skin shivers, but she doesn't feel the cold; she settles onto me as if onto a throne; I'm the territory she plants her flag in.

She spits sand, which lands in my belly button.

'The wind is blowing all the way under the water, Maman.'

'I know.'

'You can't see much, but I got you this.'

She holds out her treasure.

Two sand dollars, three urchins, a starfish with four arms.

'For your collection.'

' … Thank you.'

'And this too … '

Ama holds out an oyster. I snatch it from her, and it becomes the keeper of my secret.

I hold the shell close, press it to my manubrium, as if it were my door.

I open the oyster. There's a pearl in its belly.

I take the treasure between my fingers. The pearl is creamy and flawed.

I roll it on my tongue. It belongs to me.

Pearls are born from a wound.

Though protected by its shell, the oyster lets in a foreign body. A thin crack, a moment of inattention, an open window: the grain of sand slips inside, penetrates it, and settles under its sole defence, its shield.

The grain of sand finds itself in this new vulnerable space. It scratches it. The oyster is wounded. To protect itself, it covers the grain of sand with the nacre that makes up its shell. It gives it a bit of its body; it thins its skin to envelop the guest, which becomes a pearl. Wrapped in the oyster, it can stay.

The oyster is wounded, but it makes a treasure out of its assailant.

Ama asks me where the artist is.

I hide the pearl under my tongue and tell her I don't know.

Ama tells me that's okay.

She stands up and heads over to her father.

Her bare little back is silhouetted against the grey sky like a victor, her spine is wavy, and in it I can see barely folded wings. I'm going to lose her too.

'Wait up!'

I run to my daughter, who belongs more to the land than to me. At her feet, there's a dotted trail of baby teeth, which she follows as if she had made it herself.

Ama takes my empty, splintered, salty hand in hers, which is immense.

'Come on, Maman. Papa's waiting for us.'

I'm no longer in the habit of being incomplete. I go home, but only by half.

The men I have loved all gave me a light before leaving.

Their light still touches me.

I write at night in their shared halo.

Their flames have their own shapes and their own stories. They pulse at night, but they don't run on electricity. My lights glow with luciferin.

I have loved a lot.

No one light takes away the warmth of another.

That was true until you.

What lights me now tells the story of you.

Our happy, normal lives resume, each at their own pole.

We also exist without each other.

We can go on this way. Pretending as if.

Ama's baby tooth was left stranded under the pillow. The tooth fairy didn't come.

Will she come tomorrow?

Ama combs out the knots in the cat's fur, whose belly is growing rounder by the day.

Her voice flits through the kitchen like a little bird; she peeps out new sentences in invented colours that I can't see or hear.

I'm still soaked with you, and I can't absorb another presence; I make a lunch without music, a sandwich of mechanical gestures.

I caress without skin, I tuck Ama in with my back turned, I make love to your health.

I search for an excuse to call you.

A serious illness. Your baby in my belly. Death.

Yes, I'm ugly when I'm like this.

I hope for an accident like a baton to bust down your walls.

Janine dies before I do.

You're here, you came.

You're wearing a black leather coat, and you're talking to others louder than you talk to me.

You move wider and rounder. I want to throw myself in the path of your every movement. I want you to stumble into me. I am stock still in the midst of condolences until your abrupt laugh slides my way like an anchor. Your joy quenches me.

You harpoon me with your dark eyes, seize my skeleton, your kingdom.

I grab you by the manubrium and undress you in the columbarium.

We tremble, naked, backs against the dead.

We make a list.

– Walking arm in arm at night along the Canal Saint-Martin

– Listening to countertenors in a cornfield

– Tasting spices at the colourful counter in an alley in Jerusalem

– Kissing at the call of the muezzin

– Wandering through the galleries at the Centre Pompidou, holding hands in the bookstore on the ground floor

– Smoking hash under a weeping willow

– Making love under said willow, hearing young people drink and laugh nearby and not caring

– Making love in an alley in Maghreb

– Making love in an alley in Italy

– Making love in an alley in Portugal

– Making love in an alley in Haiti

– Reading aloud passages from a philosophy book while sitting on a dirt road, diving into a wild river, dripping onto the pages

– Exploring my grandparents' neighbourhood in Paris, and telling you about my happy childhood amidst the smell of piss and boxwood

– Going cross-country skiing, eating a piece of cold bread that I cut for you

– Sleeping in a hut lost in the winter woods, getting up to feed the fire and listening to your breath

– Visiting the 14,125 islands of the Japanese archipelago

– Climbing the 5,600 metres of Mount Damavand in Iran

– Sitting side by side in silence

You ask me whether I want to take these risks, with you.

You invite me first to follow you to a new island for the night.

But my daughter has a dance show.

I'm the caretaker of her memories.

I want her to leap headlong into my applause and be able to hang on to my pride if she stumbles.

I won't go to that island with you.

In the entrails of my tatters sleeps a ring of dried dune grass. I slip the wedding ring on my finger as I would screw a bolt on what remains of my skin. The plant breaks apart, its dam too weak for my erosion.

Ama dances among dozens of other little ballerinas, and I see her from behind my veil of tears.

She doesn't dance like the others: they're drawn to the ground whereas she's drawn to the sky. Ama isn't aerial; she is profoundly light. I love her so much.

The show is over, the lights come up, and I try to hide my smeared face.

Ama, wearing her tutu, waves to the room full of parents who are harvesting the happiness they are due. They are good parents.

I go over to my daughter.

Will she remember I was there?

My hug is awkward. Like the starfish, it's missing an arm. I wonder whether the other mothers notice.

The cat is panting, stretched out on the floor. Her belly is too heavy to carry. The tomcats come for her, wait a while on the balcony, then get fed up and go off to live at the whims of the passing hours.

She remains heavy and prostrate as she watches them go by.

I pack my bag.

Ama asks me to take her this time.

I write a line on a piece of paper, a stripe of automatic words of apology. A tightrope walker could walk them. The other words are hidden behind them. I love, I moult, I leave.

I rip up my story. I don't run, I choose myself.

Ama stops chirping; she follows my movements with her big intelligent eyes.

She comes over and gives me her tooth.

The fairy forgot again.

I kneel down in front of her.

The fairy didn't forget you, Ama.

She searches for a real answer.

It's the heart's fault.

Her eyes reflect mine.

I slip her baby tooth under my tongue.

A pearl and a child's tooth sink into my flesh.

I'm banded.

I leave.

Ama stands in the window and singes my back with her eyes.

We come from there, from the connection, we are born attached to a cord, like mountaineers, attached to a belly, a soul, guts, a voice: we come from two.

– Anne Dufourmantelle

Philosopher Anne Dufourmantelle wrote in praise of risk.

And then one afternoon, off the coast of Pampelonne, she swam out to save two drowning children.

She reached them, pushed them toward the shore, and saved them.

But her heart gave out. She stopped breathing.

The body of the fifty-three-year-old woman was fished out of the water by the father of the children she saved.

He comes back for her every year, with his children, to the beach near Ramatuelle. *We aren't trying to heal from sorrow; sorrow is the only thing that is faithful.*

I wait for you in an anonymous studio.

A room of one's own borrowed to love you.

A blue room all our own, to plan our rescue.

But you don't come.

You're afraid of drowning, and you know how to rebuild walls. You make them watertight; you protect yourself from emotions that are too intense.

We are a tidal wave.

You once told me that you won't let yourself be abandoned twice.

I didn't realize that you were announcing your departure.

You wait for me on a bench, a bouquet of colourful tulips on your lap.

I spent hours making chainmail so I could approach you.

I sit down jangling beside you.

You don't look at me when you tell me you're leaving. Going far away from me.

I've lost my voice.

My body starts ringing, unspooling a thread of sound to keep me in the world.

I'm a mummy fashioned from small metal parts who manages to look at you.

Your eyes. Your forehead. Your lips. Your beard. Your neck, your shoulders, your back.

That's where I'll go then, behind you, under your skin, hidden in your memories.

Our bodies take each other like tectonic plates colliding; we slam together and our pain gets entangled.

I keep a dead bouquet of dead tulips in memory of you.

I find a caterpillar in it. It's rolled up, frightened, and immobile. Like me.

It tells me about its trip.

A field in Amsterdam, the hold of a plane, the hands of an artist, the hands of a woman in love.

The caterpillar moves.

It's alive.

I've stopped crying; I have no water left.

I put the surviving insect in my pocket and head out in search of you.

I bought myself a red coat.

I walk with my hands in my pockets; I'm a blood stain looking for you.

I see you everywhere.

Every body is your body.

Psychiatrists say that those in mourning hallucinate the dead.

The human brain manages the violence of a loss by punctuating daily life with the presence of the beloved, until healing occurs.

You're the man crossing the road pushing an empty stroller, and the one in a window kissing a woman.

You're the man at the wheel who gestures to let me cross, and the one who speeds ups to kill me.

You're the young woman with the ethereal gait and the old man with the weight of the years in his footsteps.

You're the little green figure that lights up across the street, and I walk at your signal, drawn by your light.

You're a foot race behind me.

You're the child clinging to his mother's hand.

You're the gust of wind that already carries on it the scent of ice.

You're the dried oak leaf that falls from its branch for me to step on.

You're the flat ground beneath my feet and the space I travel through without you.

I have words to stab you with.

I have a spray of machine-gun fire for you. Bleed with me.

You have no vitality, you're so old you're almost dead, you're a coward and already almost lifeless; you're nothing like a Magi, you're no Epiphany.

Die and give me back this space, so I can fill it with something other than you. Die and give me back my joy. You don't deserve it.

My archivist body still comes, and all my orgasms are for you.
    A bouquet of violence, a pointed *fuck you.*

I love you.
    I'm a proud bleeder walking on fresh snow.
    I don't know how to push away my pain; I become my pain.
    I'm a queen, and death throes are my crown.

When I unfold, I don't walk; I float with no anchor; I see no one and no one sees me. In the store windows along the Main, beds for sale are taking some sun. I lie down on each of them. Lying in a straight line. Lying in an L. Lying in an X.

Vertical is no longer my thing.

I want nothing more to do with the sky; I curl up in a cradle, and I close my eyes.

The cat gave birth to a single kitten. She watches over it day and night, curled up in the back of a drawer.

We keep the door closed even when she wants to open it. The baby must be protected.

Our submerged island lies under the frozen river.

I search for a reflection, a finger of coral, the crumb of an island that will tell me our story. There's nothing left.

The cold grips my feet and climbs up my legs; the blue of my lips spreads through my body. I become an ice statue where our encounter is fossilizing.

I feel nothing anymore; I simply sum us up.

I close my eyes.

There's a burst of a metallic sound, and the subterranean waters start to heave. At the bottom, the bells rocked by the waves ring out, and the ice cleaves. The river gives birth onto me.

Narcisse is born from the explosion. She leans over, licks my eyes, and sucks in my pain. Her lips cover mine like fog at Easter. Narcisse lets her warm saliva run into my mouth to warm me. Her webbed hands wrap around my waist and penetrate my sex, yanking on spring to save me.

My skin splits on our eroded shores. I jettison all our tremors.

We honoured the human adventure; we lived in its maw.

Hisaé comes over to my house to stroke my hair. I cry on her waterproof skin.

She tells me about kintsugi.

I don't know what that is. She tells me it's what I should do with us.

You take a broken object and make something new from the breaks, without erasing them. It's a Japanese technique used to repair broken porcelain, which is reglued with gold.

I will melt our sutures between words; I will draw oxygen from our new punctuation marks. I will write our story.

I fill a box.

What I'm abandoning of you:

- An unfinished painting
- An Opinel knife
- A dried puffball mushroom
- An open oyster
- My manubrium in pieces

What I'm keeping of you:

- The smell of spice and the riverbed
- A pearl
- The outline of a groove on my lip
- A table in your name in the midst of a party
- The heart of a blue whale (180 kg)

I'm a ballroom where people are talking loudly, where they kiss each other on the mouth, where they dance late into the night.

I'm a ballroom, bathed in orange light, where people laugh without a net, where they share a glass. I'm a ballroom with a small wooden table in the middle of it, empty.

It's lit with two candles that never stop burning. On the tablecloth, your name is written in block letters.

Day and night, my whole life, out of the corner of my eye I will see this little table reserved for you, in the midst of a party.

I discovered a missing piece, and I know that from now on it will be part of me.

My man is in amber and granite; his perfect back is like a boulder he invites me to run aground on. At home, the windows are still open. Children are still playing outdoors.

Sadness is a new veil that covers me.
It isn't ugly or heavy, but it's foreign to me.
I go toward it.
Bonjour, tristesse.

My man is a horticulturalist who gives me a myrica gale to replant. The little bush grows like a bridge. Indigenous people attribute to it properties based on where it grows, straddling the soil and fresh water: between sleeping and waking. A tea from an infusion of its leaves fosters lucid dreaming and brings answers. I drink a cup immediately. I will put the rest in the ground, near the river.

A huge woman, draped in black silk, places my viscous heart on a scale.

If it is pure and light, I will be left to live in peace, surrounded by those I love.

The woman places a long feather as a counterweight, and my impure heart immediately plummets, dragged down by the weight of its desires.

The feather flies up into the air, and the woman glares at me and shoves my guilty heart into her mouth.

I wake up screaming.

Sacha declares a moratorium on myrica tea and makes me a double espresso.

He invites me on a trip. The giant lilies are in bloom. It's time.

I'm afraid of missing you if you come back, and I say no.

I let him go without me; I wish him a bouquet of lilies and just as many lovers. I burst into tears in front of my neighbour's messy yard, where a wild bunch of myosotis grow higgledy-piggledy, an insolent bed of forget-me-nots.

The cat got out through the open windows.

The kitten is meowing at the back of the drawer.

Ama comes to get me in the midst of my sadness: the kitten needs to be saved.

The kitten fits in my daughter's hand.

His wet nose is searching for a teat.

The young veterinarian gives me a recipe for homemade milk for the kitten; I will have to be its mother and feed it every four hours. Before hanging up, she tells me I need to close the windows, which makes me feel guilty. I guess I'm returning to the world. Sadness is giving way.

Ama feeds the little cat with a bottle.

She strokes his soft belly between each drop.

She sets her alarm clock at night and rocks him in her young arms, which already know how to love.

That night I walk through the Kyoto National Museum.

I have come to thank you for leaving. To thank you for saving us.

Thank you for Ama. Thank you for Sacha. Thank you for me.

I find your painting in a quiet corner of the museum. A blazing blue, the light of which radiates when you squint.

I see us in it.

With my fingertips I touch your name at the bottom of the water.

My back lights up. Your heat is behind me. I don't turn around.

They say a person dies twice. The first time, when they cease to exist. The second, when their name is said for the last time.

I stay silent.

I protect the imprint of your white heat, which no tear can extinguish.

I am the keeper of what you have burned into me, and I will take care of it.

I go out through the museum doors without looking back at you.

Ama is mourning the little cat.

He died on her lap; his grey eyes are open, and his coat is salted with tears.

Devastated, Ama grunts her sobs and screams her pain.

I'm with her; I stay in the background and help her. She passes through her storm.

She doesn't want my arms; she's doing battle, courageous, stormy, and alive.

On the other side of the day is the warm air of an orchard.

I pick fruit by turning it from right to left. I pick backward. My way.

The fresh lemon falls into my palm as if onto a bed.

Its skin warms mine, and its sharp smell makes my eyes water. A tacit agreement between the senses, like a dance.

It's hot. I need to drink.

The soil is dry, almost sandy.

I adjust the blue veil on my hair; I mop the sweat from my brow.

Behind me, my daughter bites deep into a lemon.

She spits a seed into her hand.

A seed, a declaration: love.

Then she does it again. Ama swallows the warm juice from the new lemon, lets it swamp her tongue and run down her throat. She winces and smiles at the same time.

My daughter has tasted life.

We're walking to school.

Ama doesn't want another cat. I get it.

She slips her hand into mine.

New skin will grow over the pain.

She will nourish herself with the pain.

And new wonders will be born from it.

A minuet in the sky. The Canada geese are returning.

Ama turns to me. If I'm still alive, I will look to the sky and to the birds disrupting it. I will shout, 'Hello, ladies!' like before, too loudly, embarrassing her.

'Do you see them, Maman?'

Ama stares at me.

She summons me back to the emergence of the world. She teaches me to read again.

In the blue light of the young day, Ama walks with an ancient gait.

'Maman, you see them?'

The geese fly past the sun, and I squint.

'Yes, I see them.'

I have no regrets.

I brandish my passions like kites.

'HELLO, LADIES!' Ama shouts.

'HELLO, LADIES!' we shout together, very, very, very loudly.

In memory of Janine Barbeau
(1928–2022)

With thanks:
Marie-Hélène Voyer, Catherine Gagnon, Fanny Noisette, Dany Dumont, Frederic Hartog, Marie-Jo Gauthier Bérubé, Vincent Delmas, Jean Bédard, Alfonso Mucci, Aimie Néron, Catherine Larivain, Ariane Riou, Alexander Reford, Sylvain Legris, Frédérique Bérubé, Léa Taillefer, Guillaume Simoneau, Gilbert Caillère, Catherine Lemay, Habitat BESIDE, La Maison d'Ariane, Alliance Fleuve St-Laurent.

Anne Dufourmantelle, Belinda Cannone, Mona Chollet.

Mélanie Vincelette, Emmanuel.
Alix, Manon, Philippe, Nadine.
Emile, Manoé, Ulysse, and Mishka.

BIBLIOGRAPHY

Cannone, Belinda. *Le Nouveau nom de l'amour*. Paris: Stock, 2020.

———. *Petit éloge du désir.* Paris: Gallimard, 2013.

———. *S'émerveiller*. Paris: Stock, 2017.

Chollet, Mona. *Reinventing Love: How the Patriarchy Sabotages Heterosexual Relations*. Susan Emanuel, translator. New York: St. Martin's Press, 2024.

De Montifaud, Marc [Marie-Amélie Chartroule]. *Madame Ducroisy*. Paris: André Sagnier, 1879.

Dufourmantelle, Anne. *Éloge du risque*. Paris: Rivages, 2021.

———. *En cas d'amour: psychopathologie de la vie amoureuse*. Paris: Rivages, 2012.

Lochmann, Arthur. *Toucher le vertige*. Paris: Flammarion, 2021. p. 206.

Murakami, Haruki. *South of the Border, West of the Sun*. Philip Gabriel, translator. New York: Knopf Doubleday Publishing Group, 2010.

Pastoureau, Michel. *Blue: The History of a Colour*. Mark Cruse, translator. Princeton: Princeton University Press, 2001.

Perrault, Pierre. *Le visage humain d'un fleuve sans estuaire*. Trois-Rivières: Écrits des Forges, 1999.

Roumain, Jacques. *Masters of the Dew*. Mercer Cook and Langston Hughes, translators. Florida: Educa Vision, 2017.

Born in 1972, and named an Artist for Peace in 2012, **Anaïs Barbeau-Lavalette** has directed several award-winning documentary features. She also directed two fiction features: *Le Ring* (2008) and *Inch'allah* (2012), which received the Fipresci Prize in Berlin. She is the author of the travelogue *Embrasser Yasser Arafat* (2011), as well as the novels *Je voudrais qu'on m'efface* (*Neighbourhood Watch*), *Femme forêt* (*To the Forest*), and the international bestseller *Le femme qui fuit* (*Suzanne*), winner of the Prix des libraires du Quebec, Prix France-Quebec, Prix de la Ville de Montreal, and shortlisted for the Best Translated Book Award and Canada Reads.

Rhonda Mullins is a Montreal-based translator who has translated many books from French into English, including Jocelyne Saucier's *And Miles To Go Before I Sleep*, Gregoire Courtois' *The Laws of the Skies*, Dominique Fortier's *Paper Houses*, and Anaïs Barbeau-Lavalette's *Suzanne*. She is a seven-time finalist for the Governor General's Literary Award for Translation, winning the award in 2015 for her translation of Jocelyne Saucier's *Twenty-One Cardinals*. Novels she has translated were contenders for CBC Canada Reads in 2015 and 2019 and one was a finalist for the 2018 Best Translated Book Award. Mullins was the inaugural literary translator in residence at Concordia University in 2018. She has been a mentor to emerging translators in the Banff International Literary Translation Program.

Typeset in Arno, ABC Prophet, and Slate.

Printed at the Coach House on bpNichol Lane in Toronto, Ontario, on Zephyr Antique Laid paper, which was manufactured, acid-free, in Saint-Jérôme, Quebec, from second-growth forests. This book was printed with vegetable-based ink on a 1973 Heidelberg KORD offset litho press. Its pages were folded on a Baumfolder, gathered by hand, bound on a Sulby Auto-Minabinda, and trimmed on a Polar single-knife cutter.

Coach House Books is situated on occupied land, the traditional territory of several Indigenous nations, including the Mississaugas of the Credit (an Anishnabek people), the Haudenosaunee Confederacy, and the Wendat and Petun nations, and now home to many First Nations, Inuit, and Métis people. This land is covered by the Dish With One Spoon Covenant, an agreement between different First Nations communities to share resources peacefully and equitably, and by the Two-Row Wampum, a covenant of mutual respect and non-interference between early settlers and the Haudenosaunee. The land is also subject to Treaty 13, sometimes called the Toronto Purchase, signed between the settler colonists and the Mississaugas of the Credit.

As a settler organization, we acknowledge that we have violated these treaties and agreements. We acknowledge the grievous and ongoing harm of colonialism, and we strive to work toward a future of justice and reconciliation.

Edited by Alana Wilcox
Cover and interior design by Crystal Sikma
Cover photograph 'Sophie dans le nuit' by Frédérique Bérubé
Author photo by Lawrence Fafard
Translator photo by Owen Egan

Coach House Books
80 bpNichol Lane
Toronto ON M5S 3J4
Canada

mail@chbooks.com
www.chbooks.com